The Case of the

Pederast's Wife

The Case of the Pederast's Wife

A Novel
by

CLARE ELFMAN

Dufour Editions

First published in the United States of America, 2000
by Dufour Editions Inc., Chester Springs, Pennsylvania 19425

Cover Photograph: Constance Wilde and Cyril, aged 5, 1889,
by permission of Williams Andrews Clark Memorial Library,
University of California, Los Angeles.

Dufour ISBN 0-8023-1332-9

Library of Congress Cataloging-in-Publication Data

Elfman, Blossom.
    The case of the pederast's wife : a novel / by Clare Elfman.
        p. cm.
    ISBN 0-8023-1332-9
    1. Wilde, Constance, 1858-1898--Fiction. 2. Wilde, Oscar,
1854- 1900--Marriage--Fiction. I. Title.

PS3555.L39 C3 1999
813'.54 21--dc21
                                                    99-044235

Printed and bound in the United States of America

To the memory of

Linda Elstad

And with appreciation to the rest of the
Sunday bunch for their help and support:
Laurel Schmidt, Durney King, Marion Zola,
Maurice Zeitlin; and to Anne Fox
for her invaluble early readings.

About the Author

Clare Elfman's interest has always been the search for love in unique settings. Her novel, *Strawberry Fields of Heaven*, explored upstate New York's Oneida religious community where all husbands were married to all wives in a frankly sexual union based on the primitive church of St. Paul. Her novels based on her experience working in the Salvation Army Home and the Crittenton Home with teenage expectant mothers won her Best of YA awards. Her screenplay on the subject of teen pregnancy won her an Emmy. She is currently working on a stage version of *The Case of the Pederast's Wife*. Clare Elfman lives in Los Angeles, California.

1

CHAPTER

Hysteria is a condition of the nervous system peculiar to females between puberty and sixty. The patient becomes suddenly insensible, falls, but generally into a chair, eyes closed, lids tremulous, limbs stretched out and spasmodically contracted, chest heaving, often a violent struggle requiring strong men to subdue even a small woman. She might put a hand to her throat, indicating the presence of a globus, a swelling which moves from the stomach and works its way up to the throat. Treatment: cold water poured on the head or down the back, whiskey or other spirits, belladonna, Indian hemp and, of course, morphia.

Dictionary of Domestic Medicine (1890)

My father's bible. I have seen him drag a woman out of the house into the yard and hold her head under the pump.

When I became a doctor, Hippocrates advised me to practice my profession with honor and to do no harm, unlike my father who was a cruel bastard and did, to my mind, enormous harm to women.

Malingerers, he called them. Used any excuse of illness to escape their responsibilities. They were *hysterical* in the Greek sense in that the sexual organs were the source of their anxieties, and the sooner those culprits came out, the better. My father pioneered the surgical technique for what he called "the salvation of women." Of course his death rate was scandalous, but not his fault. "Nature of the beast," he laughed.

Until I was thirteen, my domain was the upper floors of our four story brownstone in South Kensington. I still had the comfort of my mother's plush and velvet, lady-fern and aspidistra and soft deep feather beds. Below, forbidden, entered by a separate door, were the rooms where my father received his patients, all of them women.

On my thirteenth birthday, my father solemnly led me into his study to explain the bodily changes that had recently come over me. In reference to these: I was to keep myself "clean," my hands away from "trouble," and cold showers if I were plagued by "sick dreams." A bit late since I had been boarding at school among boys who ritually self-abused, talked of nothing but female anatomy, and read Gothic horror stories that always included naked women, bound and struggling in the hands of dastardly villains.

Now that I was privy to the secrets of manhood, and since I was to follow him in the sacred profession of medicine, it was time for me to enter the *sanctum sanctorum*. I still remember his heavy hand on my shoulder as he led me down the stairs and through that forbidden door.

The room we entered was airless, hushed, sickly carbolic. As he turned up the gaslight, I saw a long table fitted with leather restraints and metal contraptions for fixing the feet. Beside it on a rolling table, instruments so oddly shaped, silver sharp, and frighteningly intrusive that I went weak in the knees. Milky glass bottles were ominously marked with fiery flames and death heads. This was the torture chamber of my Gothic nightmares! And these razor sharp, corkscrewed, grasping things were to be the tools of my profession? I felt suddenly faint. I was scolded for being lily-livered. For some women, my father said, pain can be cathartic. He stroked his moustache. "Keeps them from malingering."

On the night before I left to begin my medical training, he invited his colleagues to a celebration dinner. They drank enough to describe to me how, on my father's first successful surgery, he passed about the excised organs on a silver plate. They found this story terribly amusing. To them the female surgery was no worse than a farmer neutering a pig.

In the spring of 1892, I received my medical degree and found myself trapped in my father's practice. The "young" Dr. Frame treated only the less important cases: morning sickness, flatulence, swollen ankles on over-weight matrons who spent the entire day doing needlework or gorging rich cakes at tea parties. I was to stay strictly away from the subject of "sheaths" or as we called them "French letters," anything that disturbed the natural rhythm of the conjugal act and thereby spoiled the husband's pleasure. And I was never to use the speculum, because women would flock to a young doctor for the pleasure of the examination alone. I was to practice my craft by applying the pessary to hold up the prolapsed uterus of older women whose bodies were worn out by childbearing, or to record complaints of vaginal discharge which were delicately called "white flowers," caused, according to my father, by sexual overstimulation or self-abuse. And of course, all cases of *hysteria* were strictly his domain.

Hysteria and *hysterical paralysis* were catch-all useless terms describing a symptom which a physician could not directly link to physical causes. When Caroline Otterman developed terrible back pains and a numbness in the legs shortly after she was jilted, my father pronounced it paralysis due to hysteria and prescribed three months bed rest, a series of energetic massages which were called *lommi-lommi*, and a daily diet, for a slender young woman with a cinched-in wasp-waist, which included (I quote from his notes): 10 ounces raw meat soup, plate of oatmeal porridge with cream, boiled egg with three slices of bread and butter, 10 ounces of milk, half pound steak and potatoes, vegetables and an omelette, fried sole, roast mutton, ending the day with potatoes and fruit, 10 ounces of milk and soup. For the crying spells, he prescribed small doses of morphia.

I knew Caroline. She was one of my set. I also knew her mother. The breasted-gorgon we used to call her. An overbearing woman who completely oppressed Caroline who used to get migraines when her mother walked into the room, and spells of asthma when her mother blamed her for something, which was often. I remembered one dinner party where some rotter had reached under the cloth and touched Caroline's leg. She ought to have jumped up and slapped his face. Instead, as she tearfully explained to me, she was certain she had done something to encourage him, she felt responsible, she stood up to run, her legs went weak and she'd fainted.

I knew why her legs were numb. Her mother was embarrassed by the broken engagement and blamed it on Caroline's inability to hold onto this gem of a fiancé. When I explained this to Caroline, she jumped to her feet in a moment of justified anger, stalked about the room, furious at her mother. And then she collapsed in tears. She had no way to escape, nothing she could do except wait for another suitor. The weakness in the legs returned, she ate her steak and potatoes, and welcomed the morphia. The only thing that calmed her, she said.

There had to be a better way to treat women. You see, I understood women. I could talk to women. My father's day was on the way out. These were modern times when madmen were being unchained, alienists had begun to categorize diseases of the brain, mesmerism was the rage, and "specialists" diagnosed by feeling bumps on the head. But nobody in London was doing the kind of work that had begun to fashion itself in my imagination. No one as yet recognized the relationship of female ailments and the female mind.

Men were direct. They saw a problem, they set about solving it. Women, on the other hand, walked labyrinthine paths to satisfy their needs. Those were the paths I had yet to explore, if I could only escape my father. When I spoke of setting up my own practice, he went tight-lipped with anger. He had paid for my food, my clothes, my medical training and by God I owed him. I supposed that he was right. And so I *listened* to his patients, made my notes, and waited my time.

Then one day Eleanor Dunston came to see me. Ronnie Dunston was a friend of the family. I had been best man at their wedding. Now less than a year later, she suffered from "white flowers," pain in menstruation, and a deep melancholy. My father had been treating her with cauterization painful enough to make her faint. Her good fortune that my father was detained at the hospital, a difficult breech delivery, dangerous not only because of the baby's position but because of the danger of "child-bed fever" which often imperiled hospital deliveries. She begged me to help her. "Martin, I've been ill almost since the honeymoon. I love Ronnie but I feel weak, I am in pain, I can barely tolerate the marital bed. I can speak to you, I cannot speak to your father. Please tell me, what is wrong with me?"

To know what was wrong I needed the speculum. Damn my father and his proscriptions. I was licensed to make my own medical decisions. I asked the housekeeper to help Eleanor into an examining robe. I had her up on the table, asked her to close her eyes and be brave, and I took a look inside. What I found was the extent of my father's maltreatment of women. Ronnie Dunston had contracted a "recreational disease" some years ago, treated by my father with mercury, which was why his teeth were so unsightly. Ronnie was pronounced cured in order to marry. He wasn't cured. And what I saw in Caroline Otterman was a full blown infection that caused her not only great pain but would prevent her from ever bearing children. The enormity of this crime, I could call it no less, I laid on the head of my father.

When he came home, I accused him of allowing Dunston to marry and destroying Caroline's life. He was livid. How dare I give that diagnosis to Dunston's wife? Did I realize that I had left him vulnerable to a legal action? He threatened to cane me. Accusations which I had stored in my heart tumbled out. He was responsible for the death of my mother. He claimed she died of a heart attack and had buried her even before writing to me. She was the most kind and gentle of women. This is the woman he had put to bed with the "rest cure," meaning rest with no stimulation, no music, no books, no stichery, just utter boredom until she decided that her household chores were preferable to this nothingness. How she must have suffered with his inflexibility and heartlessness. I think I called him an insufferable pig who tortured women. He ordered me out of his house and out of his life. And if I thought I would inherit from him, he would as soon throw the money in the Thames as give me the comfort of a penny of it. I told him what part of the underworld I consigned him to, I packed my clothes, my books and left his house that night.

First to a friend's for a week while I searched for rooms to set up a practice of my own. With a small legacy left to me by my dear mother, I was able to take a flat on Shaftesbury in the theater district, a part of the city with which I was familiar, being very fond of the stage. I set up my surgery below and I furnished modest living quarters above. Here I put out my first sign, Martin Frame, M.D., engraved on brass and fastened to the bricks of the facade. Before long, with my warm and sympathetic manner, I had attracted ladies of the chorus and ladies of the night, dancers with muscle aches, for I admit I was an expert at *lommi-lommi,* actors with laryngitis, comics with indigestion, a baritone who needed to be sobered up quickly when he had to go on for a sick friend, and an occasional sailor who had got himself cut up in a brawl.

Not much money in it, but those months were a revelation to a young doctor doing research in a new field of medicine. Remember Caroline Otterman and her hysterical paralysis? Well, Nellie Apple, who worked the ladies' room at the Athena Theater, had also been jilted by a young man who had made false promises and then broke her heart. This betrayal in no way affected her mobility. She simply took a small kitchen knife and stabbed him in a place that almost turned him into a castrato and walked away with the policeman on her good strong legs. Ladies in my neighborhood did not suffer from *hysteria.*

Here is what I had begun to discover: History was important to the treatment; keen observation was essential. This art I learned, not in a lecture hall, but from another physician named Arthur Conan Doyle who had created a character named Sherlock Holmes. I was mad for the Holmes stories. This brilliant detective taught me the skill of watching for shifts of eyes, bitten nails, emotional clues in the slope of the shoulders, in sighs, nervous coughs, and slips of the tongue. I became the Sherlock of the treatment room. I discovered that for a woman, a good cry was the best headache powder; that justifiable anger was therapeutic; that fear and a sense of entrapment could paralyze; and under conditions where there seemed no escape, the body might respond with pains in the back, the neck, intolerable migraines, digestive troubles, spots before the eyes, ringing in the ears. And most important, that many of these conditions could be treated with a "talking cure." Hadn't Shakespeare known three hundred years ago that fearful indecision could drive a man mad? If my father was the wrong man to treat women, I was the right one. I had the best of both worlds, not only a good ear but the speculum.

Between the two, women were safe with me.

And so I became an expert mesmerist, a patient listener, a Sherlock of observation. I could often predict by speaking to a patient what ailments she suffered. That trick and my passionate interest in what I called "hidden anguish and visible pain" made me a popular guest at dinner parties.

In short, I was young, free of my father's domination, my figure was pleasing to women, and I had a brilliant theory that might make my fortune. All I needed now was a significant case on which to write a paper that would astonish the medical world.

2

CHAPTER

Any male person who, in public or private, commits any act of gross indecency with another male person shall be guilty of a misdemeanour, and, being convicted thereof, shall be liable at the discretion of the court, to be imprisoned for a term not exceeding two years with or without hard labour.

From the Criminal Law Amendment
Act of 1885

Yet knowing this, Wilde sued his
lover's father for libel. What
unconscious desire for self-destruction
motivated this madness? I see examples
of my new theory everywhere around me.
I know little of homosexualism, but could
this illogical action make Wilde a
womanly man?

The color of the day was blood. Beginning with a street brawl between two sailors, one of them badly cut on the back, now the two of them were sober, their ship was leaving in an hour, I did some fast patching. Then a desperate mother brought in a fourteen year-old daughter of such sweet innocence that her situation would have made the Virgin Mary weep: raped by some brute of an uncle, pregnant with his child, her reputation destroyed if anyone were to learn the truth. The mother had attempted an abortion with a knitting needle. I barely saved the poor child from death by ex-sanguination. When I finally took off my blood-stained coat and stopped for tea, I was annoyed by a ring of the bell. I ought to have put up my notice, *The Doctor is Out*. But the caller persisted. I opened the door to a familiar face, a man of my own age, well-dressed, soft features. From where? "Robbie Ross," he said. "We met at Astracan's party the other night?" Of course. Flat Australian accent. But more than that, I remembered him by association. He was a friend of Oscar Wilde. "Sorry to bother you on a busy day, but I have an urgent request."

I brought him up to my disordered rooms. Astracan, a theatrical producer whom I had treated for hemorrhoids, had an elegant home in Belgravia to which I was often invited for excellent dinners and interesting conversation. That evening I had made a comparison in the way a playwright contrives his plots, always thinking of motivation, and the way a doctor of the mind must work backwards so to speak (like Hamlet's crab conceit) and find the motivational root of illness caused by events in the past. I used as an example Oscar Wilde and his ill-conceived libel suit. Ross had defended his friend by claiming that the accusation was untrue. The friendship between Wilde and young Douglas was merely platonic.

Well I knew otherwise. I was told by one of my ladies of the night that if I wanted the truth about Oscar Wilde, I ought to knock on the door of a flat at 13 College Street.

That section of town was her territory. The flat belonged to a man named Taylor who kept "pretty boys." They competed unfairly for her services. She had seen Wilde going in, and often leaving with young men beneath his station.

I offered Ross a cup of tea, hoping that his "urgent request" had nothing to do with the fact that he, like Wilde, was a poofter. I was not particularly sympathetic with "Uranians," as the literary ones of his kind called themselves. I watched him fidget and pace a bit before finding the courage to speak.

"Martin, I remember our conversation the night of the dinner, and your discussion of unconscious motives that might prevent a man in a critical situation from taking necessary action. You know that Wilde has dropped his libel suit."

"Busy day. I hadn't heard."

"He knew he was losing the case. He was wise to drop it. But the evidence against him was so damning that he's liable for charges serious enough to put him in prison."

"Is anyone pressing charges?"

"That's exactly my point. Nobody wants Oscar to come to trial, least of all the court since they may have to call witnesses with connections in high places."

Not surprising. A certain Lord something or other had recently been discovered, so the tabloids disclosed, in the arms of his handsome young footman.

"They've left him enough time to catch the boat train for Paris before they deliver the summons."

"And so?"

"He won't leave."

"What do you mean ... won't?"

"He's sitting in a hotel room, casually smoking a cigarette, waiting for them to deliver the warrant. Sentiment is against him. They'll throw him in prison. He must leave and he won't. And you spoke of your skill at talking with a patient and uncovering hidden motives. Martin, I beg of you. Come now. Speak to him. Reason with him. Get him out of there and onto the boat train before it leaves.

3
CHAPTER

The Rational Dress Society protests against the introduction of any fashion in dress that either deforms the figure, impedes the movements of the body, or in any way tends to injure health. It protests the wearing of tightly-fitting corsets, narrow-toed shoes and boots, heavy-weighted skirts that make exercise impossible. Total weight of clothing, excluding shoes, should not exceed seven pounds.

I supported rational dress, and I heard Wilde's wife speak at a meeting of the Rational Dress Society at which she wore not a dress but a pair of brown trousers. Shocking but impressive. I was mad for his plays, but the man himself was nauseatingly affected and I wondered then what she saw in him.

As we careened through narrow cobbled streets toward Knightsbridge, I planned my opening gambit in a game that might well save Wilde's life. I asked a worried Ross, "You have no indication of why he refuses to leave?" "His friends have begged him to go. He just sits there with his glass of Chateau Olivier and his Turkish cigarette, waiting for disaster. Could the emotional shock of the trial have left him numb? I don't think he ever expected things to go this far. Or he may simply think that because of his popularity, they wouldn't dare to convict him. His wife is with him now, trying to convince him to leave."

Now, the subject of the wife had come up only that morning when half-blind Molly, who cleaned my surgery, brought me the morning paper. WILDE TRIAL CONTINUES. "Poor thing," she said. Why "poor thing?" I asked her. "I didn't realize that you were a fan of Oscar Wilde." "Him? That booger can go straight to 'ell for all of me. It's the poor wife who breaks me 'eart' Just think of them poor children."

And the father of those two children sat calmly smoking a cigarette while the inexorable gears of the law were grinding out not only his fate but theirs.

The horse clattered to a stop outside the Cadogan Hotel. The streets were ordinarily crowded at that hour. But as we stepped out of the hansom cab, I could see that the curbs were thickly lined with carriages, horses snorting, pawing, drivers lounging, talking, smoking. "What is all this?"

"Vultures from the press, waiting to see Oscar dragged away."

Inside the hotel, I sensed the same air of curious excitement: whisperers head to head; maids carrying towels and linen, speaking low and glancing toward the stairway. "You see how it is," said Ross.

Two slender rather pale gentlemen guarded Wilde's door. One glanced at his watch. My guess, he was also afraid of missing that boat train. "Has he agreed?" Ross asked. No, Constance was pleading with him now. Ross knocked. I caught a glimpse of her as she opened the door. Ross whispered to her, made a hand gesture toward me. She nodded, closed the door again.

Ross introduced me to his nervous friends. One of them said, "So you're the 'head' man."

My reputation had preceded me. A reputation built on nothing, since I was as yet more theory than miraculous cure. But I was ready for Wilde. I would inquire as to his well being. Then meet the subject head on, explain in a quick phrase or two my concept of "hidden anguish," and put it to him that as a writer who used "unconscious motivation" in constructing his characters, could he not himself discern that invisible forces were keeping him trapped in that chair? Then I would watch and listen, hope that he would give himself away. My final argument, since the man was a flagrant egoist, would be that he owed it, if not to himself and his family, then to posterity to move his head before the ax fell.

The door opened and she stepped out, a tall slender woman in a brown costume with many gold buttons. A handsome woman in obvious distress. She stood for a moment, inward, her turmoil visible in the fast rise and fall of her breast. I confess that my curious eyes were on her. Aware of my presence, she raised a hand to arrange her hair, a thick mass of chestnut hair twisted into an ingenious pattern. A few wisps had escaped. The hand stopped mid-air, as if in her bewilderment she had forgotten her intention.

Through the partly opened door, I saw a man gesturing, heard a low voice imploring. And then I caught a glimpse of Wilde. He might have been a character in one of his plays, a man at leisure sitting knees crossed in a red velvet chair, one arm languidly over the back, the other holding a cigarette. At leisure, when his wife had probably been on her knees imploring him to save not only himself but what was left of the good name of their children. I had a whiff of heavy Turkish tobacco as the door was slammed shut.

That slam struck her like a slap in the face. She slumped back against the wall. "Icarus," she said.

Icarus? So she knew why he refused to run. This egoist of a husband considered himself a god and gods did not run for boat trains to escape the wrath of Zeus.

Robbie hastily introduced me. "Can you get him in to see Oscar?"

"An adamant no. He simply means for them to take him." She placed an imploring hand on Ross's arm. "Robbie, will they let him free on bail? They must, mustn't they? A man of Oscar's stature? If they release him, tell him that I want him to come home. Will you do that for me?"

He shrugged. "If I can. You know Oscar."

"Do I?" she asked. She took a handkerchief from her wrist and pressed it to her lips and then to a cheek flushed with the strain of the interview.

"You've done all you can. Let me see you home," said Ross.

"No, Oscar needs you. Stay with him, please."

Ross appealed to me. "Martin, would you be kind enough ... damn sorry to have brought you for nothing."

Nothing? This was a chance I would not have missed. My Sherlock Holmsian head was filled with questions. She wanted him home. Had he *been* coming home? Could a man go to these obscene houses of sexual dalliance and then go home all innocent to a wife and children? Could a man carry on publicly with a lover, and a sophisticated woman of her set be unaware? Ross gestured an apology to me and entered Wilde's room.

I offered her my arm and we walked toward the stairs. As she leaned heavily on me, I became aware of her not simply as an interesting subject but as a physical presence. I caught the faint scent of perfume mixed with body heat. What drain of emotion it must have cost her to plead with her doomed husband. And her trial was not yet over. I had thought to get her quickly to a carriage but between us and escape were those "gentlemen" of the press whose amused eyes followed us. I felt her weight sag, as if she might faint.

The Cadogan had a small restaurant. I put an arm about her and supported her toward the beveled doors. "I think a glass of wine would be in order before braving the street." But the room was crowded, noisy with raucous laughter, voices calling out, the clinking of glasses. Thankfully the waitress saw us. Women who earn their own way, like my ladies of the night, are generous to their own sex. She must have guessed the identity of my companion. She knew in her sympathetic heart what this woman was suffering. She pushed through the crush toward us. "Come, this way. I have a quiet spot." She led us quickly to a small corner table shielded by a post and a large potted plant. "A glass of good red wine for Madame," I said. And this kind soul, she gave "Madame" a look of such deep concern that it carried more warmth than the wine could possibly offer. Mrs. Wilde nodded her thanks. From across the room, a rise of laughter. "How beastly they are," she said.

"You know the press."

"Vultures. They used to feed on his clever lines. Now they laugh at his suffering."

"And you," I said. "How difficult this must be for you."

Her fingers went to her forehead, the ache of migraine visible in the furrowed brow, in the tight lips. "More difficult for the children," she said. "You cannot imagine."

"Are they old enough to understand?"

"The younger boy knows that something is wrong. Where is Poppa? he asks. From our long faces he deduced that his father robbed a bank. We laughed and made light of it. But Cyril, the older boy, he is too clever. I am frantic to know what to tell him."

"The older boy is close to his father?"

"Adores him. We had to bring him up from school before the gossip reached him. But how were we to explain to him, a child of nine. So we decided to send him to his cousins in Ireland until the trial was over, and of course he had to have a book for the train and I let a stupid nanny take him to the shops. He saw a placard, you know the filth they print. He came home weeping, and asked what the word meant."

"What did you tell him?"

She looked up, startled. "What could I tell a child that age? He couldn't possibly understand." She bit at her lip. "What would you have said?"

The kind waitress brought a bottle of wine and two glasses, poured one for Madame and left the bottle with me. I filled my own glass, trying to decide whether the question was rhetorical.

"If there is a way to explain, tell me. I am quite out of my mind trying to put this horror into words he can understand."

"Well then, I suppose I might say, in a boy's context of course, that his father had enemies. Boys understand enemies. And that these enemies were trying to discredit him and had accused him of terrible things. But that his father now had a chance to defend himself. And would, when he could, explain it to his son."

"Ought I to have said that? God forgive me, I said nothing. I put him on the train. I shall never erase from my mind the horror and confusion and fear on his face as he turned toward me through the window."

Tears glazed her eyes. She wept silently for a moment, then sniffed, swallowed, it was over. Her hand trembled as she lifted the glass. "Perhaps if I could have spoken with someone like you. But I have no one, you see. Not when friends begin to whisper behind gloved hands and say in a pitying voice, poor Constance and dear Constance. I am so tired of sticky compassion."

"At the least you'll know who your true friends are."

She held her glass in both hands and peered into the liquid, like a psychic trying to divine answers in a crystal ball. "Very wise for a young man."

"When you have a practice like mine, with women who have been battered by wretched men, with babies who have been left at my door by desperate mothers who cannot feed them, with actresses who fall madly in love with the worst rotters, one becomes wise in the ways of the world. I only want you to know that if you should need my help, I'm here. The trial is going to be a circus."

Now her eyes opened wide in a candid expression of alarm. "But he is innocent! They are sure to find him innocent!"

I was taken back by her statement. "I hope so, for your sake."

She looked apprehensively about to make certain we were not overheard. "But surely you do not believe him guilty."

I hesitated. "I must warn you. I don't give polite social answers. So you must take care what you ask."

"Then I ask again. They have charged him with a serious crime. Do you think him guilty?"

"It appears to me that the evidence was pretty strong against him."

"Appears. But you see, his whole life is appearance. Queensbury claimed not that he was ... that thing, but that he "posed as." Oscar would pose in a moment if it gained him attention. And some disgruntled actor got it in his head to get even with Oscar for some slight. Those boys were paid to testify."

I was frankly bewildered. The details of her husband's "vice" had been splattered in every tabloid: A love letter to Douglas carelessly left in the pocket of a dressing gown, found by a servant. Gifts of gold cigarette lighters to young common boys. Every London shop girl knew the truth. Yet she denied it. Why?

Suddenly the room seemed to empty. "They've taken him," she said. We rushed out onto a street filled with commotion: drivers shouting, horses snorting, cabs driving off. The "gentlemen of the press" were eager to get news of the ultimate fall of the great Oscar Wilde into print.

I hailed a carriage, helped her up into it and would have joined her but I sensed that she preferred to go alone. She held a hand out to me. "Forgive me. In all this horror I have forgotten your name."

I handed her my card. "Doctor Martin Frame, at your service."

And that is how I saw her, "framed" in the window of the cab, like a portrait hanging in a gallery. A young matron, her elegant but slightly disordered hair, fatigue in the angle of her shoulders, in the way her pale hand rested on the window ledge. And in her eyes, if the artist could capture the emotions, if I could capture them for my notes: pain, concern, bewilderment, sadness and, finally, as she held a hand out to me, gratitude. "I shan't forget your kindness." She gave an address to the driver, he pulled at the reins, a snort, a clatter, and they drove off.

I stood listening to the shouts of a doorman clearing the street in front of the hotel. And then it came back to me, what she had said as she left his room. Icarus. She knew Wilde's flaws only too well. And yet, she had braved the prying and critical eyes of the press to help this damn fool of a husband. The woman had to be made of steel.

4
CHAPTER

Notes on homosexualism:

Found at the local booksellers: cheap paperbound books with lurid covers on the subject of homogenic love, contrasexuality, homoerotism, simili-sexualism, uranism, sexual inversion, intersexuality and the third sex. A quick glance through brings a description of four types of homosexual activity: manual, oral, femoral, and anal. Femoral homosexuality is performed by the passive male partner while the active participant ejaculates into the fissure between the scrotum and the thighs. Occasionally a *pseudo-vagina* may be worn.

The trial was a circus. City streets rang with the cries of newsboys calling out bits of the latest testimony. Over breakfast you read another quip, the slippery way Wilde got out of this or that question. But not everyone was amused. At least not the coal merchant who came in to get his boil lanced. "I say hang the bloody bastard." Theater people were sympathetic. I bound up the sprained ankle for an actress who had caught her heel on a carpet edge. "How can they torture this gentle man? If some ... some banker or ... or a tradesman goes to a prostitute, no one makes a legal case of it. All he did was hire a 'renter.' I could weep my eyes out." Her friend, who had brought her in, was sure they would never convict him. Not with two of his plays still running to good audiences. They both knew the vindictive actor, a rotter named Charles Brookfield, who had vowed to get even with Wilde. Dreadful man, hired by Queensbury, they were certain.

And if they were certain, could Mrs. Wilde have been sincere in her belief that her husband had been, as Sherlock Holmes might have put it, "set up"? And how was she surviving the shock of her husband's arrest? Was Wilde let out on bail? Had he come home to her?

She was so much on my mind that when I received an invitation from Astracan, the producer, who was giving an Oscar Wilde party at his Belgravia mansion to honor the playwright and raise money for his defense, I accepted, hoping that Ross might be there and that I could glean some news of her.

When I arrived, the room was jammed with theatrical types: dramatic women in elegant finery, stout over-painted over-feathered actresses who had seen better days, men in "aesthetic" blouses looking like tall, short, or portly Hamlets, wealthy patrons of the arts who dared to support the man who had the nerve to stand up in court and describe his love letter to Douglas as a simple poem. This could be Wilde's greatest success, if only he could escape hanging. And everyone was tittering over the wry comment from Mrs. Patrick Campbell when asked about his outrageous behavior: *I don't mind where people make love as long as they don't do it in the middle of the street and frighten the horses.* The course of the evening was a series of readings from Wilde's works, a letter of support signed by friends and a silver plate to receive gifts of money to defray the costs of the trial.

I arrived in time for a hilarious rendition of the "discovery" scene from *Importance.* The protagonist had been left as an infant at the train station when his nurse mistakenly put the manuscript of her romance novel in the baby's perambulator and the baby into her capacious handbag which she left at Victoria Station. Stunned by the revelation, he asks, "What line!" And she answers, "The Brighton Line." My favorite scene. Who could indict a man who wrote lines like those? Unfortunately, they followed the scene with readings of his poems which I found sticky sentimental and I withdrew to a small study with a few others to wait out the next selection.

I poured myself a glass of wine and looked at "types," trying in my Holmsian way to decide what this one did and that one. "When the cat's away," said a low-pitched voice. The speaker pulled a chair next to mine. He held a glass of wine which he offered up to me as a toast. "So this is the man who is courting Wilde's wife."

"I beg your pardon."

"Oh, don't beg mine. I rather admire your audacity. And the woman could use a bit of cheering up. This isn't her brightest hour."

The speaker was dark, mustached, smarmy was the word that sprang to mind, rather an ugly sort. His coat was rumpled. He'd spilled wine on it. "You are confusing me with someone else."

"Come, Frame. You were seen with your arm about her waist at the Cadogan the other night The papers will pay well for a column of gossip as juicy as that."

I was steaming. "Who the hell are you?"

"A friend of Wilde's. I'm only pointing out that when you take a lady into public rooms, make sure she's not the wife of the most infamous man in London. As to poor Constance, she deserves a bit of pleasure. He's given her a hard time."

I put down my glass. "Would you like to join me outside, or would you rather I knocked you down right here."

"In here, if you don't mind. Young doctor assaults writer over assignation with Oscar Wilde's wife. I could get you on the front page of every newspaper in London." The man was drunk. He tried to brush the spilled wine from his coat with an unsteady hand.

"See here, I went to the Cadogan at the invitation of Wilde's friends. I am a physician."

"An abortionist, from what I hear. Hang about with whores and drunken sailors. A mesmerist or something like that. Oh, I don't blame Constance for taking a handsome young man to get even with Oscar. He was a rotter where she was concerned. He only married her for her bit of money. Gave her two children and never went home again." With that, he finished his drink, raised the empty glass to me and sauntered off.

Damn the bastard, and damn my stupidity. Had I compromised her with that glass of wine the other night? And was what he said true? Had Wilde married her only for the money? Then why her willingness to stand by him?

I rejoined the others. They were reading Wilde's children's stories. I wasn't in the mood for child's play. I left and walked the long way back to my rooms. The newsstands were closed but the placards announced in bold letters: OSCAR PUTS ON A SHOW FOR THE COURTS.

It must have been almost ten in the evening when I heard the knock at the door. To say that I was shocked to see a veiled woman of excellent dress standing there would have been an understatement. And then she raised her veil. "Let me in, please."

Mrs. Wilde! Alone and unchaperoned. My first thought was that I might have compromised her once already, that this visit might be misconstrued. My second thought was that nothing could keep me from finding out the reason for this late night visit.

"Robbie is waiting in the cab. I am desperate to speak with you."

"Come in, please." I led her upstairs. Wretched rooms for a lady. I rushed about for an embarrassed moment, picking up scattered clothing, unwashed dishes, books. "Is he guilty?" she asked.

To hell with the room. I put water into the kettle for a cup of tea and set it on the gas ring. "You asked me that once before." She took off her cloak and hat. Now for the first time I noticed that she had spectacular eyes, an odd shade of violet. And from the nervousness of her manner, her downcast eyes, her fast breathing, I knew exactly what she was asking me.

"I have decisions to make. I must speak with someone who can answer me candidly."

"You want to know if, in my medical opinion, your husband is a homosexual."

She passed a hand in front of her eyes. "Ahh…you see I was right to come. No one will say that word in my presence."

"Mrs. Wilde, you are the only one who can answer that question. You may not know all the details of his private life, but as a wife surely you know if the man enjoyed the pleasure of your bed."

"My friend Margaret, who is more worldly than I, says that there are men who take sexual pleasure only in the company of other men. But it isn't true of Oscar! Explain to me how a man who has loved a woman passionately could be of that … nature. Look …" She reached into her purse, rummaged around and brought out letters and cables. "Look at this! Read this and tell me that my husband is one of those men who is …who can only … I cannot even say it. Here."

She shoved a letter at me. Much read, much folded. *Dear and beloved: Here am I and you in the Antipodes. O execrable facts, that keep our lips from kissing, though our souls are one. I feel your fingers in my hair, and your cheek brushing mine ...* "And these." She showed me cables, each one filled with some loving sentiment. How he missed her presence. How much he adored her. "How does a man who takes pleasure in the sexual company of a woman suddenly change? What is the nature of this ... vice? Is it a vice? Was he out for sensation, because, oh, I could believe that of my husband. He is self-indulgent with food, with money. But surely only games, titillation. Not what they say about him. What is this thing? A dangerous kind of game or a sickness?"

Inversion wasn't my field. "I've done some reading on homosexualism but not much on pederasty."

"Meaning what?"

"Men who love pretty boys."

"And I've told you that Queensbury paid those boys to testify."

"And Douglas?"

"Douglas isn't a boy. He is a poet who came to Oscar for encouragement. He is charming and personable. We were friends of his mother's. He came to my house for dinner! I have danced with him. Played tennis with him. He pursued Oscar the way all these young poets do, a novice worshipping at the feet of an older man who has succeeded."

Her hands were trembling. She was overwrought. And the water was on the boil. I made her a cup of tea. She warmed her hands on it.

"Mrs.Wilde, listen to me. You asked for the truth and I don't play games with my patients. You've come to me for a medical opinion. You claim your husband is a normal man. A sexual husband."

"Passionate. I was pregnant just a few months after we married. And pregnant again shortly after my first son was born."

"Then he never left your bed. In all these years. I am asking frankly, as a doctor. Did he leave your bed?"

She looked into the teacup, trying to shape an answer. "He told me before we married that he had contracted an ... illness. He was treated and was well."

Damn and blast. The two year mercury cure. "And your husband claimed that there was no longer a trace of the infection."

"He would never have married, as a gentleman, without knowing that he was cured. But then suddenly, after Vyvyan was born, the infection returned. He was forced to leave my bed, for my sake. My husband is a passionate man. Could it be that he needed some ... satisfaction he could no longer get from me without fear that he would infect me? And that he sought other ways to satisfy himself? But not the way they say! The man is passionate but with a certain ... delicacy. He could never have done filthy things such as they whisper."

"What of the love letter to Douglas that they read out in court?"

"You know Oscar's poetry. Florid, some of it. Romantic. He said that it was a poem and I believe him." She turned away so that I could not see her eyes. "Tell me frankly, what is it that men do? Can they show... affection without the other? It was affection that Oscar needed. I wasn't clever enough to give it to him. He was away so often, he was busy in his own world, I had the children. I should have spoken to someone like you. There was no one. Tell me now. Could he have exchanged ... affection with young men without ... the other?"

It was what every schoolboy knew. Boys played games. And the rest I had gleaned from my quickly acquired library of salacious books. "Men can find sexual satisfaction together without insertion. There are many forms of mutual stimulation."

Her breath came short. She struggled with the concept. "Perhaps if I had been more clever ...".

"But let me also point out that a man in sexual distress,

as you seem to suggest, can find satisfaction by self-stimula-
tion which, from a medical point of view, is not the sin you
hear described from a religious point of view. God may
abhor that sin, but it's practiced constantly. Not only by boys
but by men. I have done it myself, when nature called."
    Her eyes were wide with astonishment. Truth is like clean
water. It washes away confusion. Or like iced water to a
fevered brow, shocking at first, but it does the job. She
sipped at her tea, set down the cup, clasped her hands and
by the set of her mouth I could sense that she had come to a
decision. Decision was in those violet eyes. "My husband is a
normal man. He had to leave my bed. He was always the sen-
sationalist. You know Oscar. Anything to shock. I believe he
went to these ... places ... for the titillation. But then Douglas
threw himself at Oscar. He is a thoroughly attractive boy.
One cannot help taking to him. He took advantage of a man
in sexual distress, and then destroyed him." She pushed
away the teacup. "I owe you a debt I can never repay. There
is no one who could have made me understand as you have.
God bless you for what you have done for me." She pinned
on her hat. I held her cape for her. For a brief moment she
leaned back as if to rest on my strength. "Surely they will see
that Queensbury meant to destroy him. I have had to send
my children abroad. As soon as my husband is exonerated, I
will join them and take them to Switzerland where my
brother lives. He has always been fond of Oscar. Once we
are finished with this ugliness, once I have my husband back
in my arms, perhaps I will find the courage to speak with
him as we have spoken tonight."
    "... one more thing. Mrs. Wilde ..."
    "... my name is Constance. You have been so good a
friend to me that no formality can ever come between us. I
don't know how I can thank you."
    "Then, Constance , let me warn you about this fallacy of
the two-year cure. With an infection of your husband's sort,
the mercury treatment does not always assure that the condition is gone. If you do choose to live with him again,

make certain that he uses a French letter. You can get good sheaths in Europe. A woman can easily find a cap, but avoid these hastily contrived sponges, they make them of fine wool or flax, with a string for withdrawal. They are not effective. Try the Dutch cap."

She lowered her veil. I walked her down the steps and onto the street. The horse was restless, striking the street with a hoof. I helped her into the carriage.

Robbie Ross was not there.

5

CHAPTER

Martin: I am devastated and cannot keep our appointment for this evening. They have closed down "The Importance" as well as "An Ideal Husband." I cannot stop weeping and I am a mere under-study. Both plays were showing to full houses. Has London gone totally mad?

Alma Belmont

Astracan had been fortunate enough to get a seat for the trial. He attended each session, and each evening met with his friends at dinner to report the latest quips and banter. "The man is a performer. He went to the States and lectured rough cowboys on *The House Beautiful* and they threw their hats in the air and carried him on their shoulders. I saw him take a curtain call dangling a cigarette from his fingers, a rather supercilious smile as if to say, You think me a genius and you are quite right. The man thrives in front of an audience. And now he's got not only all of London but half the civilized world watching his performance. Here is this bewigged barrister, an Irishman himself, mind you, someone Wilde actually knew as a boy, looking more like an actor than the actors in Oscar's plays, asking provocative questions with a straight face, and Oscar answering as calmly as if he were at one of his wife's at-homes:

Have you given cigarette cases to young men?
Yes.
Was the conversation of these young men literary?
No, but I was gratified by their admiration.
What pleasure could you find in the society of boys beneath your social station?
I make no social distinctions,
"Which is absolutely true," said Astracan. "Part of Oscar's charm."
The boys, what did you do with them?
I read them my plays.
You, a successful literary man, wished to obtain praise from these boys?
Praise from anyone is delightful. Praise from literary people is often tainted with criticism.
In reference to the Savoy Hotel evidence, is it true that the masseur and the chambermaid saw the boys in your room?
Entirely untrue. No one was there.
Do you deny that the bed linen was soiled?

*I do not examine the bed linen when I arise. I am not
a housemaid.*
"I tell you the man will walk out of that courtroom vin-
dicated. This will be his finest literary success."
"Impossible," I said. "Unconscious" forces had held
Wilde in the chair at the Cadogan and the same "unconscious" forces would drag him to ruination. This was as certain as gravity and the tides. What were those forces? That I
did not know any more than I could actually describe gravity except by demonstration. But I knew the end of that
drama as if I had sat in the audience and watched it. There
was no "deus ex machina" to save a man whose "unconscious" was determined to do him harm.
    Astracan wagered me fifty pounds that Oscar would
walk away a free man. I didn't take the bet. I did not
approve of stealing from friends.
    It was late in the day when Astracan came knocking at my
surgery door in tears. "He was inches away from freedom,
inches, but he must have been worn out. He let down his
guard for an instant and they were on him with questions:"
You didn't kiss that boy?
I gave him gifts. But kiss him? Certainly not.
And you didn't kiss the other boy?"
    "Martin, at that moment I saw the fatigue on his face, a
little glistening of perspiration. He let out a profound sigh
of exhaustion."   -
Certainly not. I would never kiss a boy that ugly.
    "The moment he said it he awoke, his fingers fluttered,
like a writer aware that he's made a mistake and eager to
correct it. But there was no pen in his hand. He slipped
into a crevice so deep that no rope can pull him out."
    What destructive forces swirled in that genius brain I
could not surmise. What worried me was his wife. How did
she survive the shock of the newsboy's cries of WILDE
GUILTY! SENTENCED TO TWO YEARS AT HARD LABOR.
    How much of a shock I realized when, in the midst of a
busy morning, I received a note from Ross, delivered by

messenger. *She must see you before she leaves. Please meet us 33 Tite Street, but come to the rear of the house though Paradise Walk.*

I knew Paradise Walk, a scabby street in Chelsea which led to the Royal Hospital, with its procession of sick, helpless, and hopeless. Tite Street which backed up to it, on the other hand, had been gentrified by artists and writers, the "aesthetic" crowd. It was the place to go, said my actresses, if you were fortunate enough to get an invitation. There were peacock feathers fixed into the ceiling, and the wainscoting was a shockingly delightful yellow and white. Now I would see it for myself, but under the worst of circumstances.

I hailed a small gondola and ordered the driver to fly to Chelsea. Crawl would be more apt on a busy London morning. We maneuvered around hay carts and brewer's drays. We were stopped at Hyde Park corner, a cart of vegetables had overturned. Beggars caught up handfuls. The driver tried to force them away with his whip. I anguished until we moved a sluggish south toward the river. Finally Tite Street, which was a row of modest houses.

When the driver approached 33, he called to me, "Something going on!" A crowd was gathering on the street. Two police wagons maneuvered to find space at the curb.

"Around the corner. See if there is an alley in the rear." Trash cans, milk delivery boxes, and a brougham, the driver trying to control his nervous horse. Ross came running from the back garden toward it, carrying an armload of manuscripts and books. "Wait here!" I called to my driver. I hopped down and followed Ross who had deposited his load and was rushing back to the house. "What's wrong?"

"Quick, before they break down the door." Into the servants' entrance, down into the kitchen and then up into the first floor hallway. "Queensbury's had Oscar declared bankrupt. They've come to strip the house. We're saving what we can before they get in."

What I saw, rushing through the house to get to her, was

white, white and light, sun streaming in the back windows, in contrast with the rest of London, all polished mahogany and heavy velvet drapery. I stood for an astonished moment at the doorway to her dining room which faced onto the back garden. White lacquered chairs and white carpet, bright blue tiles. "I'm trying to save the manuscripts," said Ross. "She's upstairs in her bedroom. Help her!"

Up the stairs, no time to look at peacock feathers. Her bedroom door was open. On the bed she'd piled clothes, furs, a box of jewelry. "Take them, quickly," she begged me. I loaded my arms, made a quick run down, outside, to the brougham. Ross was throwing books and manuscripts willy nilly onto the seats.

I ran back up to her bedroom, found her slumped on the edge of the bed, bewildered. I could hear the thumping on the downstairs door. "Why?" she asked. "What have I done to deserve this?"

What she'd done was marry the wrong man.

She ran her fingers across an exquisitely embroidered coverlet. "I made this, every stitch is mine. Martin, what am I to do?"

"Take what you can quickly." I scooped up clothing, she took books from her bedside and the bookends which must have been dear to her. She stopped at the door of her drawing room. "My guest book!" She pointed to the leather-bound book sitting on a table. I took it, picked up clothing that fell in her wake as she descended. As we reached the back door, the vultures entered the front. She stumbled, almost fell. I held onto her as we made our way through the garden and shoved the rest of her things into the brougham. Ross was breathing heavily with exhaustion. "I took what I could, but his presentation books are still in there."

"My letters!" she said. "Martin, in my bedroom, a little blue case. Hurry, please!"

I ran back into the house but it was too late. Like locusts they were stripping the place. Pictures taken down, books, ornaments, I saw one of the officers carrying down a filled carton, her embroidered coverlet and on it the little blue case. "These are only personal letters. Let me take them to her." He warned me away. This was official business. I stood for a moment, watching them carry away her world. I saw a burly mustached policeman balancing a huge box of blocks, trains, lead soldiers: her children's toys. As I walked back to the carriage, I thought, If you want to destroy a woman, this is the way to do it.

She had taken over my little gondola. "I'm sorry about the letters," I said. "They refused to let me have them." She slumped back, defeated. "What will you do now?"

"The children are waiting for me in Paris. I must join them. God help me, Martin. Pray for me." She signaled the driver to move on. "Quickly!" she shouted.

I joined Ross at the overloaded carriage. "They carried off her children's toys. Heartless to torture a woman that way. Wilde deserves to be put on the rack for what he's done to her."

"I beg you, don't wish him any worse that he's suffering now. And trust me, he had no intention of hurting her. He's terribly fond of his wife. But he was so involved in his muddle with Bosie that he didn't realize how ill she was. She's in constant pain. Has she told you?"

No, she hadn't told me, but shouldn't I have predicted it? "Pain in the back and legs?"

"She has told you, then."

"No. When did this begin?"

"She fell, at the beginning of the scandal. Caught her heel in a carpet tread and tumbled down the stairs. She's been in agony. Do you remember that day at the Cadogan? She was scheduled for surgery then, but she expected Oscar to come home. She put it off. Haven't you seen her limping?"

"Stairs? Ordinary household stairs? Carpeted stairs?"

"Yes, I think so. Something pressing on a nerve, she said."

Perhaps there was something pressing on a nerve, perhaps not. I would guess not. Not under the circumstances.

Not from what I knew of the woman. "Look, when will you be hearing from her?"

"No idea. She's on her way to the station."

"Will you be writing to her?"

"If she lets me know where she is."

"Tell her not to consider surgery until she speaks with me. It's imperative. Especially not surgery near the spine. More than imperative, critical." I looked at my pocket watch. "Any chance of my catching her before the train leaves?"

"Unlikely. She'll barely make it as it is." He climbed into the carriage, trying to arrange the mess of stuff. I sat up with the driver and we pulled away just as the police came streaming out of the back door, waving angrily at us. But our driver was skilled at the chase. He careened around corners, down alleys, and we made it safely back to Hyde Park corner. I jumped down. I would find my way back to Shaftesbury. Robbie intended to leave her things with her family, and then try to see Oscar, if he could. "It's been bad enough for him. How on earth will he survive this, knowing what they've done to her."

I made my way through the crowded streets: hawkers with their little trays peddling elixirs; men spilling out of and shoving into taverns. As I passed the theater where *Importance* had been playing, I saw workmen pulling down the billboards. I passed the Shakespeare Book Vendors. Books were stacked on the sidewalk table, all of them Wilde's. "What's going on?" I asked a gentleman who was quickly sorting through and choosing.

"Pulling his books off the shelves. Take a few before they're gone. Ought to be worth something if the bugger dies in prison."

As soon as I reached my surgery, I began to record my first notes in a therapy that I knew would revolutionize the treatment of women. Here was a woman who had been cruelly punished for her husband's crime. He had been proved guilty; yet she denied his guilt. She had been faithful through the trial; now she was forced to run to save her children. Her husband; her children. How could her body not respond in pain? And I knew, without a doubt, that once the nervous excitement was over, her legs would feel the numbness of entrapment.

If I had been waiting for a perfect subject, I had found her. I also knew that this woman was in hell, and that I was destined to be her salvation.

With a flourish, since I knew this notebook would one day be of enormous importance, I wrote on the opening page in the style of Sherlock Holmes:

The Case of the Pederast's Wife.

6
CHAPTER

The root of neurosis lies in a childhood sexual abuse in its rudest form, rape by a father or sexual encounters with a brother or even abuse by a lascivious nursemaid...the problem then: Find the historical truth. Go back, caput Nili, *find the source of the Nile. The physician leads the patient carefully back to childhood memories, listens for mneumic clues, watches for visible signs, not unlike an archeologist digging with pickaxe and shovel, searching out old inscriptions in ancient stone.* Saca loquuntur. *Stones talk.*

S. Freud (1896)

I did not expect the urgent command from my father. The hand-delivered note read: *I expect you here at noon. Without fail.* No other explanation. Filled with curiosity and undiminished anger, I complied. Simply climbing the steps of the house brought me back to apprehensions of my childhood. My father awaited me in his study. I was frankly shocked at the change in him. Gaunt, sunken eyes, the heightened color not of health but of fever. He sat in his favorite chair, a rug across his knees, but his size seemed to have diminished. In a voice as cold as ice, he asked me: "Have you had enough of your little experiment? Are you ready to come home?"

"Not at all. I am perfectly happy as I am."

"I am dying," he said. "I have an inoperable cancer of the bladder. I haven't long to live. You are to come home at once and take over my practice. I will move upstairs with a nurse to care for me. You will not be bothered by my presence, and I shall die quietly. If the pain becomes too severe, I will take enough morphia to kill myself. Have you anything to say?"

What was I to say? That I was crushed and heartbroken at this terrible news? My response was as cold as his command, less feeling than if he had been a stranger. One can pity a stranger. But he had been cruel to my mother, who was always unhappy except when I was with her. She had died without the comfort of my presence.

"And so?" he said.

"As you wish."

I closed my practice, amid great lamentation from my patients who were loathe to give up the convenience of a sympathetic doctor in their own territory. And so I came home, not to his house, but to my mother's, for with his presence banished from the common rooms, her spirit returned in the little pug dogs and souvenir cups which still rested on the mantle, the crocheted antimacassars on the backs of chairs, doilies under flowerpots, embroidered verses in frames on the wall, reminders of her dear presence.

In three months he was dead, leaving me the house, the practice, and a rather large sum of money.

It was here Ross found me. He was about to leave for Lake Como to visit his mother. He had heard from a mutual friend that Constance had suffered a brutal time on her arrival abroad. Her landlord discovered her identity and, afraid to bring notoriety to his hotel, had cruelly demanded that she leave. Ross wasn't sure where Constance was at the moment but he had, through friends, urged her to write to me and sent along my request that she delay any surgery until she heard from me.

A week or so later, her letter was forwarded to me.

My dear Martin: I arrived to find that the stupid nurse I engaged to guard my children had flagrantly neglected them. She fed them nothing but sugar buns on the crossing, so they gleefully told me. In Paris, she become a religious fanatic, bought a fortune in candles and set them about the whole room. And then locked the boys in while she went out to visit friends. There were complaints against her when I arrived at the pension in Switzerland. My poor sons. They fairly leaped into my arms.

I dismissed her immediately. I was so happy to be with them at last. And I had not realized the extent of my exhaustion. The boys, released, were free to run and play and I lay back to consider what Oscar had done to us. There are two countesses who have rooms here, two old women who fled Russia and now live in rather shabby gentility. I think they never change their clothes and their rooms are kept quite dark but they adore Cyril and Vyvyan, give them sweets and all sorts of attention, and they are enormously kind to me. The boys have already been lost twice. They climbed all the way up the mountains and could not find their way down. We had beaters out with flaming torches to rescue them. I cannot find it in me to berate them. And so they go about their pranks and games and I take tea with my two kind old ladies who tell me stories of Russia and their golden days. And I think, is this how I will end my days? Moving from place to place, trying to escape from scandal? Becoming odd in little ways like these two kind old women? And what do I do? Nothing but lie here on the musty velvet sofa between the two old countesses with their powdered faces, and their wispy hair, and let them stroke me like a pet cat and feed me cups of tea which they pour from a lovely samovar. Soon I will go to my brother and let him make decisions for me. I am too numb to think clearly. Robbie said that he spoke to you of the pain in my back. And now the pain has traveled down to my legs. But I take your counsel and will wait a bit for the surgery. I will send you my brother's address as soon as I am settled. I would welcome your letter. Yours has been a clean true voice. I ought to have listened. Ever, Constance.

Since this was a new life for me, I set about erasing my father's presence from the house. Down with the heavy drapes to let in the light. I furnished an interview room upstairs where I could speak with my patients in a more personal atmosphere. I decided to grow a mustache and a beard. They came in golden and softer than I would have wished. But the effect gave me some stature. I dreadfully missed my ladies. A few ventured out of their little corner of Shaftesbury Street to my posh new offices. But now I began to attract some of the young women of my father's practice who recommended me to their friends since I was, shall I say, accessible and sympathetic.

I waited for another letter which might give me an address. I received a disquieting note from a friend in Germany. I had asked him to search out a certain Dr. S. Freud to find out if our research followed similar lines. He wrote that this Freud was a brilliant neurologist but that his abuse theory was sheer nonsense and nothing like my own concept of "hidden anguish." The Austrian's cases were esoteric. I, on the other hand, was concerned with ordinary women who suffered ordinary but often debilitating conditions: the pain in the back, weakness in the legs, migraine, digestive disorder, and, most important, a kind of deadly rationalization that drew women toward self-destructive decisions. But the Austrian's work was substantial and I ought to consider publishing as soon as possible.

I watched for her letters. I wondered if she had already filed for divorce. For a man to divorce his wife, all that was necessary was simple adultery, but for a woman, adultery had to be coupled with an additional offense. Incestuous adultery, bigamy with adultery, bestiality and so on. Wilde had given her enough aggravating circumstance. Adultery with fish and chips boys bought, so they said, with gold cigarette cases should have been ample cause. And once she was free of him, it would be easier for me to convince her to take what I called "treatment by logic." A talking cure.

I was shocked to receive her note, this time with a return address. Shocked not by the change of name. Constance Holland. Of course she needed a certain anonymity. I was shocked by her gullibility.

My dear Martin: You cannot believe how circumstances have changed for Oscar. He has had time to think in that terrible place. He understands now what he has lost by his foolish behavior. He says that he loves no one but me and the children.

I read that line again and again. An easy regret from a man trapped in a prison cell. And she believed him?

My lawyer came all the way to Switzerland to bring me his letter. Even the prison authorities were touched by it. They all feel that I am the only one who can save him now. Save him from what? I can hear you ask. My dear Martin, your voice and your counsel are with me. I know what you would say. He is like Humpty Dumpty. Can he be put back together again? My family rail at me night and day to divorce him. His friends and some of mine say that he needs me dreadfully. I will not desert him. Of course I must think of my children, and for their sake I must make a legal separation, to get control of my own money. But I shall not divorce him. And if he is sincerely contrite, I shall be waiting for him when he is released from prison. Faithfully, your friend, Constance.

To which I answered immediately:

How well you know my voice. It is the voice of logic. I am certain that your woman's heart beats in sympathy for your husband's suffering. But in my own frank fashion, I must point out that he brought this down on his own head. Are you feeling well? How is the back?

I was gratified to have a prompt answer:

My dear and good friend: Life is not as simple as you would make it. He writes as often as the prison authorities will permit, asking about his sons. He adores the boys and is sick at heart for the grief he has caused them and me. He only wants me to take a small chalet in Switzerland where he can recover and begin to write again. Thank you for asking about my back. I am more concerned with Cyril, however. That lovely boy has gone crooked in the shoulders and bent over. They say it is his sudden growth. I know that it is not. My dear Martin, we were forced to change his name. You are the only one who can under-stand the terrible grief this has caused me. My brother pre-vailed on me to understand that there could be no career for Cyril with the name Wilde. He does agree that if Oscar comes out of prison to me, and if we were to move let us say to Italy for ten years and if he would begin to write and make his reputation again, then perhaps we might some day return to England. But until then, my poor Cyril must take a new identity. We called him into the room. He knew something was amiss. His face was quite pale. My brother Otho said that from this day forward, he was not to be called Wilde but Holland, which is a family name. The look on his face, Martin. Otho said that we were to take all the name tags from his school clothes and from his books. And that never was he to mention to his new school friends that his name was Wilde. He was now Cyril Holland. He stood there, what little color in his face

*drained. He went dead white, and then he turned and fled
to the summer house. He locked himself in and would not
come out. I pleaded with him. He stayed in there through
the whole day and through the night. He would not come
out to eat, he would not speak to me. I was beside myself.
Finally I beat at the door, weeping, I could not bear it. At
last he opened the door. Tears dry. Face cold. He was not
the same boy. He had changed. And now he stoops in the
shoulders. Martin, what am I to do?*

I wrote immediately:

*My dear Constance: Consider the blow the boy has suf-
fered. Be gentle with him. Tell him that one day his father
will come back to explain. Until then, give him phosphate
of chalk and exercise. And what of your back? Of your
pain? Realize also what a terrible blow each of these
events has caused you and be kind to yourself. Take fresh
air, find a good spa, hot baths would be beneficial, and
take massage for the weak muscles of your legs and back.
Your faithful friend, M.*

And she answered:

*My dear Martin: A brief note. Leaving for Italy to be
near my dear friend, Margaret Brooke. Your advice on
massage was excellent. I do feel much better. How I wish
you were here to talk with me. I feel as though we have
known each other forever. Yours, Constance.*

The next note came, unexpectedly, from Robbie Ross.
Would I come at once to the Chelsea apartments of Lady
Wilde, Oscar's mother. She had heard of me through
Constance and desperately needed to see me.

The mother? What on earth could the mother want
with me?

7
CHAPTER

Ah, she was a beauty. Famous for it. They called her Speranza. This was the time of the troubles and she wrote a fiery letter to the papers: Go to your guns, she wrote, take up the fight for freedom. Sedition, they said. The thing came to trial, wrong man was blamed and Sperenza, she jumped up in front of the courtroom and cried: I wrote that letter. She was a tall women, gorgeous face and figure. Now Wilde was a short man, brilliant and famous, for ears, it was, that was how the boy got the name Oscar, after King Oscar treated by the father. Brilliant man, mind you, not very clean. There was this joke they told. Why does Dr. Wilde has black fingernails? From scratching himself. The man was a devil with women. Not only had a mistress but three bastard children. The wife knew about it, but she carried herself like a queen, if you know what I mean. Wouldn't soil her hands with it. Well he began to carry on with a young thing, tired of her, threw her over. Gave her money to go abroad but she was a bad penny, kept coming back. Finally when she couldn't get more from him, she let it out that he had given her ether and raped her on the examina-

*tion table. Had handbills printed up and hired boys
to pass them around. What did Wilde do? Nothing.
Not a bloody thing. But Lady Wilde, she was not one
to let an insult pass. She was great for social teas
and all that. So the woman wrote a terrible letter to
the girl's father, accusing the daughter of being a
whore. The father had the good sense to put the letter away hoping the thing would blow over. Girl
found the letter and sued for libel. Lady Wilde, she
managed the whole thing. Nobody would dirty the
name of Wilde while she was living. Dr. Wilde, he
never showed up in court. Wouldn't testify. He lost
the case, the girl got only a farthing in damages.
That's what they thought of her virtue. But he had to
stand the court costs. Well it took something out of
the man. He went off to his country place at
Moytura, to his fishing and all that. He was grand
at the fishing. Wrote books about it. His practice, it
went to the bastard son. Everyone knew about it. It
was no secret in Dublin.*

... this over a pint in the White Swan, from
a chap who knew them in the "auld days."

The woman who had been the beautiful "Speranza" was seated in a great high-backed chair, like a queen on a throne. The drapes were drawn so that the room was swamped in a funereal gloom, lighted only with candles. I understood why. She had lost the famous beauty and gone to fat. The candles were meant to soften the effect, I suppose. As she beckoned me toward her, I saw a woman grossly overdressed, layers of clothing, collars and laces, beads, medallions, pins, her hair adulterated with feathers and other decorations. The hand she held out to me was meant to be kissed. I did so with no great pleasure. "So you are the brilliant young doctor Constance has mentioned in her letters."

I thought, how sad to see a glorious warrior in the service of freedom sitting like a queen bee, sluggish, unsavory and, now, of course, with her son disgraced and in prison, what was left for her. "At your service, Madame."

"My son's wife has written to me of your kindness. And now I am about to take advantage of your goodness for a favor of my own." She held a rather tortured lace handkerchief in a pudgy arthritic hand. "You know what they have done to my son."

I wanted to say, what your son has done to himself. But out of courtesy, I held my tongue and waited.

"They are crucifying him. Because of his genius. Because he has shown them all the folly of their petty lives."

I said nothing. To my mind, when a man knows the law and considers himself above it, he subjects himself to its slings and arrows. The validity of the law aside, he knew the price before he "bought the goods."

"I wanted him to go into Parliament," she said. "He would have been marvelous in politics. Have you ever heard him speak? Eloquent. As I was once."

Yes, Madame. Was I here to be her audience? What was the point?

"He is, like me, above the commonplace."

"The commonplace."

"It was the way I brought him up. I have two sons, Dr. Frame. Only one was destined for greatness." Now she reached out and gripped my wrist with that fat damp hand. "My son and I," she said, "we understand the meaning of honor. We do not avoid our fate. We rush headlong to meet it."

The woman was living in some romantic novel. Had she been thinner and still beautiful, she might have been lying on her chaise striking meloncholic attitudes to be painted by Burne-Jones. It would have taken a painter with a great sense of irony to do her as she was now.

"My son is a genius," she said, "and genius has its privileges. He must experience, he must know sensation, he must love above the commonplace." She hit her breast with a fat fist. "My own husband had a lover and three children. When he lay dying, my maid rushed to tell me that a woman in black had come up the stairs and entered my husband's room. And I said, Let her come. I understood the grand gesture. My son and I, we were made for grand gestures and deep emotions. But I knew that his genius would send him out into a hostile world and I wanted to see him anchored. It was I who chose Constance, you know."

"How so?"

"He had to marry. His mind was in the stars; his emotions were still a boy's. He fell in love, he was rejected. I saw how his heart was broken. He was too vulnerable. Marry, I said. Settle down, I said. And then let your pen soar to the heavens. She was a beautiful girl, gentle, bright, and she adored him. I sought her out. I encouraged him. Even now she will stand by him."

"Madame," I asked her, "what is it you want of me."

I sensed the onset of tears. "I am ill. My heart is failing. I must see my son. They must grant him a leave from prison to see his dying mother."

So there it was. But why me? I had no influence. An unknown doctor, no prestigious practice. But probably everyone else had refused her and she was desperate. "Is your heart failing, Madame? Or do you simply want to see your son released from prison?"

She closed her eyes. She held a wrist out to me. Her face was puffy, almost porcine. The woman had not moved her body for years, but sat stuffing herself with sweets. I wouldn't doubt that her heart was failing. I felt her pulse, which was indeed erratic.

"Lady Wilde," I began, " I don't know what weight a letter from me would carry, but I will write to the prison authorities urging them to allow you a visit."

She took my hand in her two damp hands, the twisted handkerchief pressing my skin. "Thank you."

I had questions I wanted to ask, about the marriage, about her son, and it was not good manners that prevented me. I did not prize good manners. What stopped me was that the room was crushing me. I felt claustrophobic. Not only the gloom and the airlessness, but the hopelessness.

Madness, I thought as I walked out of that house and into the light. There exactly was proof of my theory. This woman had once been beautiful, self-willed, energetic. What "hidden anguish" had caused this "visible" self-destructive condition? Marriage to a man who had a mistress and three children? And she made so much of the dramatic gesture, *I am above the commonplace.* But was she? Or did that betrayal secretly gnaw at her heart? Did she in some way blame herself? And blaming herself, or hungering for a love that seemed to be lavishly spread about to other women, did she eat herself into this caricature? I thought, and this was to become the backbone of my theory: Why do women choose to deceive themselves? She needed that marriage and so she chose to ignore what harm it was doing her. In my mind I planned a chapter of my paper on *self-deceiving women.* And how did that self-deception translate to her son, a brilliant young poet with a lovely wife and two beautiful children. *I am above the commonplace.* What had she passed on to the son? Wilde had choices. If he had the homosexual urge, why not handle it as others had? Quietly taken himself a lover and preserved his home, the reputation of his loyal wife and the name which had been wrenched bleeding from the heart of his child. And Constance. A handsome woman with money of her own. No question, she had been dragged into the worst scandal of the century. But what prevented her from simply divorcing him and making a life for her children? Who would have dared condemn her. The world would have understood. She claimed to be the "constant wife." If that were true, she would have walked into that prison, head high, legs strong, told him she had decided to take him back and come out like Joan of Arc. But she didn't. She couldn't take him back; she couldn't walk away. Her body stopped her. It was as clear to me as it would have been to Holmes. Her husband would eventually be released from prison. And she intended to take him to her bosom and nurture him back to health? I bet my reputation and my future that she ... not *would* not, but *could* not.

It was the plot of a Shakespearean tragedy. I knew the first four acts. But the conclusion? I was the *deus ex machina*. I only had to wait for the exact moment to enter the scene. I was damned excited. My heart churned with it. I had to find a way to bring Wilde's wife back to health and sanity. Not only for her sake, but for the sake of all women who had come to the fork in the road, one leading to health and joy, the other to a life of self-inflicted wounds and physical pain. In this was I also like Icarus?

The difference between me and Wilde was that my motives were pure.

At least so I thought at the green age of twenty eight, striding down a crowded London street like a young warrior in golden armor about to enter the battle under a heroic banner, selfless, courageous, the god of good sense and logic on my side.

I sent a letter on behalf of Lady Wilde to the prison authorities.

I rushed to the mail with each delivery hoping for a letter with an Italian postmark from Constance Holland. None came.

A few weeks later, Ross sent me a note asking me to dine. At last, news of her. No, he had heard nothing from Constance. But Lady Wilde was dead. She was refused a visit from her son. She took to her bed, turned her face to the wall and died.

I received the cable a week later.

His beloved mother is dead. I cannot bear to think that this crushing news be brought to him by cold prison authorities. I am returning for a few days and will see you if I can.

8
CHAPTER

Loveless marriages are horrible. But there is one thing worse than an absolutely loveless marriage. A marriage in which there is love, but only on one side; faith, but only on one side; devotion but on one side only, and in which of the two hearts one is sure to be broken.

Oscar Wilde, *An Ideal Husband*

He himself had written it. A foreshadowing?

It was a cold Spring morning. I warmed my hands before treating one of my favorite patients, Alma Belmont, a young actress struggling to make a life in the theater, rushing from reading to reading with no success other than as an occasional understudy. One crushing disappointment after the other but being of strong spirit, she survived. How then did she put food on her table while waiting for her success? She made what choices were available to her. I will not call it prostitution, but she chose carefully a few men whom she sent to me first for examination. She was a fair actress and a magnificent lover; I know this because I was one of those men. I had no desire to marry, at least there was no one in my set who interested me. Not women who undressed in their closet and came blushing and faint to the arms of their ardent husbands and then "suffered through it." I was a passionate man. She was sweet and bright and, above all, in good clean health. And so for an occasional evening, I tended to her muscular strains, her back was often "out" and she benefited by my skill at massage. A pert little sparrow of a girl, and great fun in bed.

She was in my surgery, on her stomach, while I worked tense back muscles, tight in anticipation of an important reading that might get her a juicy part. She may have been my occasional lover, but in respect I had my housekeeper standing by to make certain the proprieties were observed, that the sheet that covered her did not slip inappropriately. She turned her sweet smile toward me. "Dr. Frame, you are a gentleman."

"Only when I am with a lady." I could feel those muscles relaxing under the heels of my hands.

The bell rang. "Have we an appointment this next hour, Mrs. Bridey?"

"Not that I know, Doctor Frame."

"See who it is." My patient lay decorously on her stomach, and Mrs. Bridey felt it safe to answer the door. Once the chaperone was gone, my little actress dropped the sheet, sat up, stretched, ah what a body she had. "I feel absolutely wonderful. I will get this part, Martin, see if I don't."

Mrs. Bridey returned. "A Mrs. Holland to see you."

She was here. "Quick. Bring her up."

My little actress pursed those clever lips in a stagy *moue.* "Ah, someone special? Don't tell me you have found a better lover?"

I slapped her fanny. "There is no better in London. This is a friend in trouble. Be an angel and go by the side door."

She dressed in front of me, a pleasure to watch. She buttoned her coat, pinned on her hat and was about to leave when Mrs. Bridey knocked and led in my guest. Constance, thinking us alone, lifted her veil. I gestured for my little actress to get the blazes out of there but she hesitated, uncertain, and then, horrified me by saying, "Mrs. Wilde?"

Constance was shocked.

Alma held out a hand. "Forgive me, but we met when I was understudy for Cecily in *Importance,* and I have thought about you so often."

Constance, to my amazement, accepted the hand. "Miss Belmont. You were kind enough to take my older boy over to the sweets table when we came to rehearsal."

"I only intruded ... because ..." Suddenly tears came to her eyes. "I was at the theater the night you came in with the two of them. I thought at that moment you were the bravest woman I had ever met. I had to tell you because you have been so much in my heart. Your husband is a good and gentle man, and I pray that you get through this ... I am saying this stupidly."

Constance embraced her. "You could not have said anything that would have pleased me more. I have just come from the prison. If you had seen what I saw, you would have wept rivers. Please keep my husband in your heart."

Now my little actress became flustered at her own audacity. She squeezed Constance's hand and fled.

"I am so sorry." I said.

"About what? It was the kindest gesture I've had since

arriving in London. They would not let me see him alone. I had to stand there, like a common burglar's wife, and tell my husband that his mother was dead."

As I led her down the hallway, she was visibly limping. A good fire burned in the library hearth. I took her hat and coat, called for Mrs. Bridey to make some tea, poured her a sherry. "Tell me, how is Italy?"

"I've taken an apartment near my friend in Nervi. I have found a gem of a housekeeper. The weather has been beautiful. I've felt well enough to take a short walk now and then."

"... well enough to take a short walk *then* and now your back aches like the devil, your leg pains you and your right hand feels numb."

"What sort of wizard are you, Martin?"

"Not even a parlor trick. I don't know any other woman who could have done what you have just done. Walked into a prison with courage that would have made the Madonna proud. But your mind says yes and your body says no. Your mind says to your legs, Here is the prison door, walk in. Your legs reply, Run like the blazes and get out of here. And as you sit there, holding your wine glass in your left hand, you clench and unclench the fingers of your right hand."

She touched those nervous fingers to her forehead.

"And you have a dreadful migraine. Would you like some powders? Or better, let me massage it for you." I didn't wait for an answer. I sat beside her, turned her away from me and with my strong fingers, which I confess are very clever, I began to work the brow, and then behind the head, and then the muscles of the neck until I heard her sigh of relief.

She fell against my shoulder. "I am constantly in your debt."

"Tell me what Miss Belmont was talking about. What happened to make you the bravest woman she has ever met."

She lay back against the sofa, her eyes closed, that thick mass of chestnut hair, the throat, the rise and fall of her bosom, the air of ineffable sadness. "When he came to tell me that he was suing for libel and needed my help, when finally I saw that the years of waiting were over ..."

"... waiting for what?"

"I always knew that when the madness was over, he would come back to me."

"He needed your help for what?"

"He had to raise money for the lawsuit." She opened her eyes. "Must you sound so judgmental?"

" It is a doctor's prerogative to make judgments."

"You are not my doctor, you are my friend. And perhaps I am also a wizard. You think my only way out of this maze is for me to separate from my husband, and you are wrong."

"Good lord, am I as transparent as that?"

"You don't understand that he left me in the same way an opium addict falls deeper and deeper into hell. Finally the madness was over. He was abjectly sorry. He had risked our good name and now he was going to do something to regain it. I offered to help him raise money."

"And what did she mean by your being 'between them'? Between who?"

"Now that the libel was out, we would have to dispel the vicious gossip about Bosie Douglas and my husband."

"And ..."

"... and he asked me to go to the theater with them so that the world would know that Bosie was no more than a family friend."

"Good God, woman. You went to the theater with your husband and his lover?"

She drew back as if I'd slapped her. "Don't you ever call him that! He was never a lover. I was the lover. He was the devil, the tempter." Then she took my hand in her two hands as if to anchor me so that I would understand. " Martin, have you ever gone through St. Gothard's tunnel? On the way to Switzerland? That dreadfully long tunnel?"

"Yes, once, when I was a boy."

"You go into darkness and the lights come on and the porters come through and put buffing around the windows so that the cinders cannot get in and you ride along in that awful darkness and the air becomes closer and closer, the tunnel seems never to end, and then the heat of the engines begins to fill the tunnel and the cinders find their way through the chinks in the windows and children in other carriages begin to cry out in fear and the tightness clutches you and you pray for the tunnel to be over and it is never over, it goes on and on and just when you think you will surely faint, you see a bit of light, you have been saved and you come out into the sunlight. Oscar is in that tunnel and there is no end and there is no light. They brought him to me in his prison clothes, his head shaved, his hands a mass of scars where they have him picking oakum or some horrid thing. He has been trapped in that cell except for a short walk in the prison yard, and even then he is forbidden to speak with the other prisoners. I begged them for a moment alone with my husband. They refused. I wanted to comfort him and we couldn't even touch. You know that I am in hell, but at least there are moments of respite. I have a sweet apartment, a housekeeper who pampers me, I see the children during holidays."

"I seem to be missing a piece of your story. That evening at the theater. Something else happened."

"You probe with a very sharp scalpel."

"Then tell me not as a doctor but as a friend who loves you and wants to see you well. What happened that night at the theater? You expected him to come home penitent, fall to his knees and ask forgiveness."

"I hoped for that, yes."

"And he disappointed you."

"He kissed me and thanked me and said that he had to prepare his case and that he and Douglas were going off to Algiers."

"After everything you had sacrificed, he left you."

"... to prepare his case."

"And then ..."

"... I went upstairs, changed. I was still in shock from the emotion of the evening. And then I heard the bell. Who on earth would call at that hour? I knew it was Oscar. He had realized what he had done and he had returned. I rushed to comb out my hair, I put on my best robe, I pulled on slippers, but I must have missed a strap and I ran downstairs ..."

"... and you caught your heel and fell."

No answer. I knew. She was not as good an actress as my little friend. She gave it all away. " Stay in London for a while, here with me. Let me work on that back."

"How I wish I could, but I am on my way to Victoria Station. My bags are in the carriage downstairs. I take the afternoon boat train. I desperately need to be home in my own garden."

"Then let me see you to the train."

"Yes. Please."

We rode silently through the London streets, her face social and impassive. How women manage. Hair arranged, clothes arranged, face painted, and in her heart she was being torn between wild horses. "You really think you can put Humpty Dumpty together again."

"I am the only one who can. Sometimes a woman does an intricate piece of work and only too late discovers that some threads have been wrongly sewn and she must go back and unravel the whole, bit by intricate bit, to redo it. I am caught in a bad piece of work."

Why was it *her* needlework and not *his* design? Part of the story was missing.

Victoria Station was crowded, smoky, noisy. She was in pain, limping noticeably. I kept my arm about her until she reached her compartment. I helped her in, settled her, put up her traveling case. And she said, "Is Miss Belmont your lover?"

"My what?"

She pulled me down beside her. "You ask me all sort of

enormously personal questions as a friend, not a doctor. Well as a friend, I am curious. Is she your lover?"

I couldn't help smiling. "Occasionally."

"Is she a good lover?"

"Actually, yes."

"And without her, your life would have an emptiness in it."

"An emptiness of sorts, yes, I suppose so."

I heard the whistle. Time to leave the train. "Martin," she said, "my husband was a magnificent lover. Think about it."

I stood, collected my hat. "As a playwright your husband is certainly unique, but the world is full of magnificent lovers." I kissed her hand. She held onto my hand for a moment, and reached up and touched my face.

The meaning of that moment I was not in a position to understand.

9
CHAPTER

Regarding S. Freud:

I do not believe in the importance of heredity as much as in the importance of familial behavior, such as natural affection, parental love and, conversely, the absence of love during the formative stage.

He says: Even an innocuous experience can be heightened into a determining force if the subject is in a hypnoid state. How in ordinary daily intercourse does a patient end up in a hypnoid state?

I feel free, as a fellow scientist, to borrow from Freud. I also invite S. Freud to borrow from me when I deliver my paper on Hidden Anguish and Visible Pain in the treatment of the common ailments of women.

*D*ear Martin, Yes, I do feel somewhat better for the massage and the short strolls down verdant country lanes. My back still pains me, however. And I have met this absolutely adorable little village doctor who has assured me that a small surgery will lift the tiny bone which is pressing on a nerve and causing me this pain. Yes, I have been writing to Oscar. My husband has learned such painful lessons. He tells me that there is a reason for all suffering and this terrible chapter in his life was sent to him by God to teach him what is important in his life. He has not only forsaken his wife and beloved children in his search for titillation and sensation, he has turned his back on his art and for an artist, that is unforgivable. Yes, if he continues to improve in this manner, I will take him back. I am the only one who can save him now! From what, I wanted to ask her. What more could he possibly do to destroy himself? He only dreams of the small chalet in Switzerland where he will heal his body and spirit in the warm security of his family. He misses his boys terribly.

I cabled my answer. At all costs, avoid little village doctors who claim that surgery on the spine is only a small procedure. I have never had the opportunity to examine your back. Please allow me to visit you at my own expense and give you another opinion of your condition. If my theory is right, I may be able to cure you without surgery which is dreadfully dangerous.

She answered in a light mood. I have heard from Robbie of your "talking cure."

I assure you that I could talk myself hoarse and my back will still pain me. But I understand your concern and I love you for it.

I cabled her again. Then do this for me. Wait until your husband is released from prison. I promise you, when you see him again, you will know immediately whether the cure for your pain lies in the careful use of question and answer in the calm atmosphere of your own home, or *under the harsh light of a primitive operating theater and the dangerous scalpel of a little village doctor.* She humored me. *Whether talk can cure or not, I do miss your voice and your good common sense. I wish you were here. The roses have bloomed early, the room is filled with them. And I will take your advice and the suggestion, which I admit astonished me coming from such a realist as yourself, that I will be cured by the warm affection of my husband returned to me. Have you so much changed?* She misunderstood me completely.

I decided not to elaborate but to wait for her next letter. Nothing. I cabled my concern. *Just give me news of your health and well being.* No answer. I tried to locate Robbie Ross. He was abroad. In desperation I went to Astracan, my producer friend, whose lachrymose expression told me that something was terribly amiss. He sent down to his cellar for a bottle of good wine, we sat on the broad veranda overlooking his formal gardens, and when we had mellowed with a few glasses, he told me the story of what had happened.

"You remember the bankruptcy? One of the assets was a Life Interest in her estate. It could be bought back in favor of the children and that she intended to do. But his friends, Martin, his so-called friends, they were afraid he would not be back on his feet for God knew how long, and they did not want him to starve, so they put some pounds together and made an offer for the Life Interest in Wilde's behalf. When she heard of it, she went mad. How could he claim that money for himself when it belonged to his children.

She wrote accusing him; he denied it totally. He knew nothing of the affair. His friends made the offer without telling him. He swears it was without his knowledge. Well, she can't be sure, can she?"

"What do you think?"

"Martin, I love Oscar. He's a genius with the pen but with money...I wouldn't put it past him."

"But he denies it."

"Absolutely."

"And she doesn't believe him."

"She says she does, but I've heard from a few friends who have visited her at that charming apartment in Nervi that she is unsure. And she's ill. And Oscar is about to be let out and she's promised to meet him when he arrives at Dieppe. A grand mess, if you ask me. Whoever made that move with the Life Interest ought to be horsewhipped."

Wilde would be coming out, and I knew without a shadow of a doubt that she would not see him. She could not. Her legs would not let her.

The curtain was about to come up on the fifth act of this Greek tragedy.

Or Greek comedy, with its cuckolded husbands and amorous wives. Was he a great man flawed? Dragging tragedy onto himself because he defied the gods? Did humorous dialogue in a play make a man great? He had written other more serious work; I had never read it. Perhaps he was a genius. But I thought of his son on the train to Dublin, knowing that his father had done something so hideously shameful. To tear apart a child's faith that way. How could he have done it? What possessed him to betray innocent children who relied on his strength and support? And Wilde was so bloody flamboyant and theatrical about the trial. No, this whole affair was too sordid for tragedy. Comedy then, but she wasn't laughing, was she. Neither was I.

Wilde was released from prison in late spring.

Astracan brought me the story. Robbie Ross and other friends met him at the prison gate. He had survived hell. He came out thinner but still Oscar, smartly dressed, hair perfectly arranged, and in relatively good spirits.

"And his wife? Did she meet him in Dieppe?"

He mopped at his brow. "The wife was too ill to join him. Oscar was terribly upset, but willing to wait as she promised to join him soon."

I wrote to her again. No answer.

I wrote to Margaret Brooke, who Ross advised me, happened to be the Ranee of Serawak. The "white" Rajah governed some dark skinned people, but the Ranee lived in Italy. What was I to call her? I settled on Madame. Was Constance well? Because if something were wrong, I would leave on an instant for Genoa.

It was Constance herself who wrote to me: *I was too ill to meet with him. But it was I who paid for his first meal in the free world. I will see him as soon as I am able.*

This I related to Astracan who shook his head in despair. "Martin, everyone paid for Oscar's first meal in the free world. He has enough money to last him for three years if he's careful, but when was Oscar ever careful?"

Nothing more for a month. Finally a letter. Not in her hand but typed badly on a typewriting machine.

Summer in Nervi is hot but tolerable. How I wish you could see my garden. The cabbage roses are open, will go to seed early and the ground is strewn with rose petals. The flowers are so profuse, it seems a fairyland. If only I felt well. The pain is intense, not only the back but my legs as well. They sometimes feel numb. My hand is now so bad that I have bought this typewriting machine which I have not yet mastered. I have seen Cyril and Vyvyan, we had a sweet visit. I have been tempted to go ahead with the surgery, my little village doctor warns me not to wait too long. My only concern is that I wish to bring Oscar here to me at Nervi and surgery means weeks of recuperation and I do not wish him to be forced to cope with that, he has suffered so much already. Yes, I know what your comment would be in response to what I have said, but if you love me, dear friend, do not utter it. I am very nervous at the prospect of seeing him but I know how anxious he is to return to a stable life and that is what I was always able to provide for him. So we will see. And if you are right, and if my back and legs miraculously improve when I am in his dear presence again, I will send you a bottle of champagne and you will toast us. I do not expect to live with him as man and wife, not until I am assured that certain elements of his life have changed, but to shelter him and nurture him as his mother might have done, to let his children play at his feet and hold him and kiss his dear face, that is what I envision. If he is as I pray he will be, I will send him immediately on the search for the perfect little chalet and you will finally visit us here, and see how wrong you were about my husband.

Finally you will meet the real Oscar Wilde.

The news came from Robbie, bitterly. "He's gone back to Douglas."

"When? What happened when he met with her?"

"She never met with him. I can't say what happened."

I cabled that if I did not hear from her, I was coming to Genoa. Finally she wrote, on the typing machine, a letter filled with error and overstrikes. *"Do you believe in one's fortune showing in the lines of the hand? My dear Mrs. Robinson read my hand after the trial. She said that once it was all over, I would find happiness again. I expect the hand also lies. Please do not come now. I am in too bad a mood for visitors. Perhaps in the Spring. Give me some time."* The signature was shaky.

I advised her to have massage and to spend time in the sun. I had a card from a spa where she was taking the waters. She was thinking of me and wished me well. Cyril had much improved. She was sad that the children had to be separated into different schools but Vyvyan was such a soft child, she had sent him to the Jesuits in Monaco where her dear friend, Princess Alice, would look in on him from time to time, and Cyril who was all sports and competition was back in school in Germany. Nothing of Wilde.

I had two more short letters, neither of them mentioned her health. It was this book and that poem she wished me to read, it would add dimension to my scientific mind, and she missed me.

I was forced to write: Were the legs better? Was she ailing? Nothing in return except a Christmas card. And then finally in early spring, an alarming letter. And a more alarming cable.

Martin, I have destroyed him. The return address, her friend Margaret Brooke's, in Genoa. Followed by a cable from Margaret Brooke, the Ranee herself. *Constance has spoken of you so often, I also think of you as a friend. She intends to go into surgery with the local butcher. Imperative that you dissuade her. Please come immediately.*

I reread the cable as my hansom cab rattled through the streets toward Victoria Station. I hurried the driver. I had to catch the boat train.

"Off to Paris for a bit of fun, guv'ner?" he asked.

Nothing so frivolous. I was a warrior off to rescue a woman in distress. And through her all women destined by their "unconscious wounds" to lead disordered tragic lives.

Someone had to be *deus ex machina.* Why not Martin Frame?

10
CHAPTER

Notes for a lecture:

...the pitching of the ship and the turbulent waters were no more chaotic than the turbulence in my heart. I was on my way to treat my first patient. I had come with no metal instruments nor hellish cauterizing irons of my father's medieval practice. I came only with the sharp scalpel of my mind. I remembered my first dissection, the corpse of a woman who had died simply of "hard times." Through her I learned the heart, the lungs, the liver, the little finger-shaped appendix, the arteries, the veins, the convolutions of the brain. I thought, if only I could dissect and analyze the mind of a woman...

When I left England, London was bone cold and dead gray. Genoa, as I walked out of the train station, was also gray but of a warm hazy early morning mist. And as I climbed into a carriage for the long ride to the Ranee's villa, the mist burned away to an astonishing clarity of light. A different sort of light. A soft easiness was what I sensed as the little horse began his climb up a gravelled road bordered by twisted cypress and untended margins. We passed fields with great masses of weed and flower cohabiting together, as if the gardener had succumbed to a drunken lapse of judgment. Below us was a wide sweep of the Mediterranean coast and sloping olive groves with that same soft definition between grove and fields of daisies. Soft, soft. I could see why she chose Italy, away from the clearly defined borders of British life. I warned myself to take care. One needed clearly defined borders. This was seductive country.

When finally the horse stopped before the Ranee's villa, the driver leaped down, gathered up my travelling case, smiling and bowing me to the door. I did not find this charming, but rather obsequious. As I sifted through the strange coins to pay him, I evidently didn't choose enough. He pointed to another coin, which I assumed to be an expected gratuity. He bowed and smiled himself back to the carriage. This informality, I supposed, was part of the charm of this country.

I rang the bell. The door was opened by a little gnome of a maid who spoke no English. I handed her my card. She peered at it, and then exclaimed, "Dottore!" and led me to a sitting room that could only be Italy. Chairs and sofas of light materials, flowers and pots of thick blooming leaves, and through the open window a view of a spring garden that might have been painted by one of the moderns, with masses of color spilling into and over each other, the white to the blue, the green fern to the red petalled cabbage roses, the early-blooming roses Constance had spoken of. I took the letter out of my pocket and read again the words: *Martin, I have destroyed him.* What in this bucolic setting could have caused such distress?

"Doctor Frame!" The woman who entered the room was perhaps fifty, stylishly dressed, mannish, square jawed and very direct. She held a strong hand out to me. "I didn't expect you until this evening."

"I was able to catch the Orient Express in Milan. I came straight through. How is she?"

She motioned me to a chair. "She hasn't left her bed for a week. She eats nothing. She lies in the dark and prays to her dead grandmother."

"I received a desperate message from her. What happened?"

"What has been happening for two years and she is too blind to see it. Perhaps she'll tell you. She won't tell me. Friends have come by, his friends I should say. She has always been gracious to them. Now she refuses to see anyone."

"They pressure her to take him back. She's torn between loyalty and reality."

"You understand the situation. But this surgery is not the cure. Not under the knife of that hideous creature in the village. I've found a competent surgeon for her in Zurich. This village doctor is a charlatan."

"And if she doesn't need a surgeon."

"She is in terrible pain. I hear her cry out."

I touched my breast. "It is possible, just *possible*, that the pain is not in her back but here." I touched my head. "And here."

"But I assure you, the pain is genuine. She's not a dissembler."

"The pain is absolutely genuine. Her husband committed a crime; she paid the price. And the price is pain and paralysis but the kind of pain that might be lifted without surgery. Because of certain, let me call them emotional scars, her mind has become corrupted with misinformation. Her impulses are false. If she goes to a local butcher, it's not for surgery but for suicide, and you must have seen it or you wouldn't have called on me."

She opened a silver cigarette case, offered me one. I declined. "She wrote two letters. They seemed too much like farewell letters. She made me rush out to post them."

"One to her husband and one to her older son."

She peered oddly at me. She was probably short sighted. "How on earth did you know?"

"She forgives the husband, and she asks the son to forgive his father. She's ready to throw her life away and all she thinks about is the husband. Does that strike you odd?"

She took a cigarette from the case and lit it herself. "This ... misinformation. How do you cure her of that?"

"We talk. I ask questions. She answers. I interpret and try to bring out the truth. As simple as that. No hocus pocus, if that's what concerns you."

"Questions of a private nature."

"The most private."

"And this is a cure you have tried many times before with success."

"Not on a subject whose symptoms are as clear and dramatic as hers but I am confident ..."

"Then you intend to use her as a guinea pig. "

"At the least I can keep her from a deadly surgery. At best I will have her on her feet again."

"Has she known this about you? That you want to treat her?"

"She knows me as a friend. She knows of my work but never considered it for herself. You want to save her from the local butcher? I am the other choice. If I fail, you can always take her to Zurich. But even with a skilled surgeon, surgery on the spine is a terrible risk. Trust me, this treatment can only do her good."

Her eyes were searching me out. "But she is more than a subject ... you care for her."

"Good God, woman, of course I care for her. I've just suffered a bad crossing, seasick most of the time, I sat up in an overnight train that had no bedroom for me, I have drunk coffee that tasted like mud and eaten food heavy enough to give me colic for a week. I need a good strong cup of tea and a hot bath but I will forgo both of them if you will just show me to her room. She is sinking into an abyss. Let me get her out of it. "

She closed her eyes, considering. Then she looked at me, hard. "I knew someone like you. Determined, full of spirit, self-assured. He was the rajah of a dark-skinned people in a God-forsaken land which suffers a terrible heat and withers until the monsoon. He needed a wife of means to be his companion and to help him survive in that poor country, and so he married me and brought me to Serawak. I loved his spirit and his strength. What I found once there was a pompous clay god of a wretched kingdom where the subjects bowed and scraped the ground as their white rajah passed by. I suffered not only the terrible heat but his impossible demands. One day as I prayed for the rains to come, rocking on the hammock trying to escape that dreadful sun, I heard the patter of rain. I thought, at last. I turned. It was only the Rajah of Serawak passing water on the verandah. I packed my trunk and left. A man may not be what he seems at first. Had he been gentle and loving, I would have followed him to the ends of the earth."

"But you've made my point for me. You found yourself in a bad situation, you packed your trunk and left. Nothing ambiguous about your decision. Now, why isn't she able to make the same unambiguous decision? I care for the woman as much as you do. I want nothing more than to have her on her feet again, without pain, to know that there is still a life ahead of her. It breaks my heart to think of her children. If anything should happen to her, what would become of them."

"... ah the poor children." She rubbed out the burning end of the cigarette in a potted plant. "I can't see into your head to judge your motives and I don't know your work enough to judge your competence. But you do care for her.

If you can help her out of this pit of despair, you will have my undying gratitude. But if you have other motives than the ones you have described to me, and if she is hurt by this, God help you."

"I take your warning as concern from a loving friend. May I see her now?"

She led me down a hallway to a closed door. She raised a hand to knock. I stopped her. "Don't give her a chance to refuse my visit. Just let me go in to her."

She pursed her lips, raised her brows, looked me over yet once again and shrugged.

"Very well, you are the doctor."

11
CHAPTER

Consider:

1. The history.

2. The sexual connection, not because of the Austrian, but because her husband's crime was of a sexual nature and knowing the full extent of his "sins" she still considered returning to him.

3. My own brusque nature. I must be careful to temper my natural enthusiasm in deference to her weakened condition. On the other hand, isn't my enthusiasm necessary to drag her out of the abyss? I travel without a map of an uncharted territory.

The room was airless, drapes drawn, swamped in gloom. She lay deep in a four-poster, hair unbound, spread like dark seaweed across the white of the pillow. I felt exactly as I had in Lady Wilde's room, crushed by the odor of illness and despair. I pulled open the drapes. Light flooded the room. I opened a window. In rushed the sweet morning air.

She stirred, she turned, she threw up a hand against the light. Chalky pale, eyes dulled from a long sick sleep, it was a moment before she recognized the reality of my presence.

"Martin? Is that Martin?"

"I left as soon as I received your letter. Just arrived."

Her eyes were dull with something deeper and darker than sleep. She turned and tried to sit up against the pillows, crying out in pain as she moved.

"How long have you been suffering like this?"

"Too long. A small piece of bone is pressing on the nerve. A simple operation. A few moments on the table, I may be free of pain. Martin, I am beyond suffering. I have no choice."

"I've come. I am the choice."

A wan smile. "My dear friend. I never meant for you to come all this way but oh, I am so grateful to have you here." She tried again to sit up, crying out against the sharpness of the pain.

"Let me help you." Gently I lifted her up against the pillow. I kissed her hands, cold hands, I warmed them in mine. "I ought to have come sooner."

"Martin," she said, wincing as she turned toward me, "you don't know what I've done."

"Yes, you told me. You destroyed your husband. You are a destructive woman, selfish and self-involved. You think of no one but yourself."

Tears glazed her eyes. "I'm ill. Don't tease with me."

"Tease? My dear girl, do you think I've come to amuse you? When was the last time you were on your feet?" I didn't wait for an answer. "Permit me." I turned back the covers and ran my fingers down the backs of her legs. Flaccid. The muscles were dying from lack of exercise. And the feet, cold and dry. Very cold. I rubbed them to restore the circulation. "Would you like some tea before we begin?"

"Begin what?"

"The talking cure."

"You intend to play parlor games to cheer me up. You cannot know how ill I am."

"I may be the only one who does know. This game takes no energy at all. Just relax, lie there and talk to me. I'll sit beside the bed and listen."

"Talk when I can't keep two thoughts together. I do nothing but cry. You don't want to deal with a weeping woman."

"Crying washes out the eyes. Shall we begin with childhood memories?"

She pressed her palms to the sides of her head, which must have been splitting with migraine. "Childhood? I've been lying here praying to God to protect my children when I'm gone. I cannot play your games no matter how well you mean them."

"There are games and games. You say you've destroyed your husband. I need to know how. I need childhood memories because I want to know the child who grew up into the woman who married your husband. Do you understand me?"

"My husband." She blinked, thought for a moment, and like a swimmer having yielded herself up to drowning, reconsidered death and came up from the dark underworld. "If you know the child, you mean, you will come to know the woman. And then you'll understand the wife. And the truth of what I have done!"

"Exactly."

Her fingers pulled nervously at the bedcovers. "And if you find out that I did destroy him."

"Then we find a way to make amends."

She simply came to life. Her eyes, the tension in her body, the gesture of her hand. "Amends ... is that possible?"

"Everything is possible in the light of day. Nothing is possible from down there in the darkness of despair."

She pushed back her hair where it had fallen over her eyes. "You want to know me as a child, to help you understand why I married him and how I have mortally wounded him now."

"Exactly. Before I call your maid to bring your tea, not only will you understand my method but you'll be eager to continue. Now, as a child ... just say what comes into your mind."

"Nothing comes to my mind."

"The first word. Start with a word, a phrase that describes the child."

"Martin, I am ill. I cannot do this."

"Of course you can. Just a phrase. Humor me."

"Sad eyes. I had sad eyes."

"Sad eyes. What caused these sad eyes?"

"My mother ...no... please don't call her back to me now when I am so low."

" Just trust me. You didn't get along with your mother."

"She disliked me. She was at me all the time."

"At you how?"

"How ... it was Constance this and Constance that. Constance, you are so stupid. Constance you are not helpful. Can you do nothing right? Why did you wear mauve when it makes you look pasty instead of the blue which I laid out for you."

"... but why?"

"Please, I can't do this."

"You'd rather lie there in pain thinking of nothing but how you destroyed the man you once loved? Humor me. Tell me about your father."

She ran a hand through her wild hair, pushing it away from her eyes. "My father. My father and I were very close, and whenever he was home, which was not very often, he loved to be with me and that she couldn't bear."

"He was away on business."

"He ran with the Prince of Wales' crowd. I think he ran with other women."

"You knew this."

"Yes, I think so."

"And as a child you understood what that meant. Running with women."

"I understood that my father loved other women more than he loved my mother. Who could blame him. She was cruel."

"Did *you* feel that in some way his interest in you was to blame?"

"I? I don't remember. It was a dark, sad time for me. I only know that when my father died and I was left alone with her, she was so beastly to me that my brother went to my grandfather and begged him to take me in. Martin, please ..."

"Just go on. You're doing splendidly. Did your grandfather take you in?"

"Yes."

"Yes and...?"

"And gave me an allowance and a dowry, so that I would not have to marry out of desperation. As far as the implications of 'other women,' it was not until I heard about grandfather and the scandal in the Temple Gardens that I had any idea of what men *did* with women."

"What on earth happened in the Temple Gardens?"

"He was a barrister. He worked fourteen hours a day and the poor thing snapped. He exposed himself to some nursemaids in the park."

"Was your grandfather charged?"

"I think so, but none of the nursemaids would testify. I think they were more amused than aroused. And when we came to live with grandfather and looked at the roly poly old thing at breakfast having his eggs and bacon, and thinking of what he had done, we used to laugh behind our hands."

"But you were happy at your grandfather's?"

"As happy as one could be in a house of solid mahogany and a stern aunt who ran it for him."

"Were there other men who courted you before Wilde?"

She put her hands to her hair. "I must look wretched. Give me a mirror."

"Your hair is fine. Was Wilde your first love?"

"No, I had received proposals but I had no intention of marrying into my grandfather's world."

"What world was that?"

"Law and stuffy parlors and my Aunt Emily's little teas with women in black balancing teacups and talking about their indigestion. I loved the Irish side, that was my mother's family, all laughter and good spirits. All except for her."

"... so even as a hurt girl, you knew what you wanted."

"Did I? I suppose so. Whenever I was really wretched, my father would take me away to Babbacombe Cliffs where he had a dear friend. It was the first time I'd seen what a true home could be. She lived the aesthetic life, a house of color and light and walls filled with Burne-Jones and Rosetti. I recall running through those halls simply on fire with joy. As if my heart had been locked away and suddenly my prison doors had opened." She closed her eyes in recollection. "Or like coming out of purgatory into heaven. I would have died for a house like hers. Color and light. That is what Oscar preached."

"You met him how?"

"His family in Dublin were part of my family's social set. He had met my brother Otho. And when Otho went off to Oxford, all we heard of was Oscar this and Oscar that. Oscar set upon by bullies and fighting his way out. Oscar taking prizes. And Oscar's brilliant papers. I thought, how romantic."

"You thought Wilde romantic?"

"You only see him in hindsight. He was handsome and dashing and his voice, he had a resonant voice that thrilled to the heart. Then my Aunt Ella came to visit my mother and since she was quite friendly with the Wildes, she suggested asking Oscar to tea. We almost swooned, my cousins and I, the thought of the famous Oscar Wilde coming to tea. We were mad with excitement."

"You never found him affected."

"It was a pose. Oh, sometimes when he was nervous. He was never affected with me."

"So here is what you've said to me. You were made to feel damn guilty by your mother because she was jealous that your father loved you and did not love her. He ran with other women, so to your childish mind, if a father does not find love at home, it was acceptable to love other women. Your grandfather had, shall we call it a sexual episode which you found amusing. You were infatuated with the aesthetic movement and when you met your husband, all this was in your history."

A blush colored her cheeks. Her eyes brightened. "...but that's all true!"

"So you see, this isn't a child's game."

"This is your talking cure?"

"No tricks, nothing up my sleeve, simple logic. Like a jigsaw puzzle. You put together all the pieces and you see the true picture."

"Yes, I see what you are doing. Yes."

"Then quickly, before I have your housekeeper fix you a lovely tea, tell me about this man you say you've destroyed. Go back, remeber the days when you loved and sustained him. Tell me about the grand love affair."

"When I first loved him? When he became my life?"

"Yes. When you were happily in love. When you became *his* life."

She relaxed against the pillow but turned her eyes away from me. "We were the younger set. Trapped in deadly parlors and whale bone bustles and corded leg-o-mutton sleeves. And here was the famous Oscar Wilde come to free us. Let the weight of your clothes hang from the shoulders, he would preach. Loosen the stays! We were mad for it. His gospel was light and color. Oh I wanted that. And his voice, it thrilled to the soul. And I was in the very room with him, taking tea with him. I watched him from where I stood with my cousins. He turned and caught my eye. I blushed with embarrassment and he saw me and smiled. I quickly walked away but sure that his eyes were following me. Me! He had the most beautiful women in London at his feet and his eyes followed me."

"Yes, I can quite see why."

"Can you? I wasn't a beauty. Pretty enough, I suppose. I wore clothes well. But I was so pitifully shy. I was sitting at the piano when I became aware of this ... presence over me, watching my hands. I was so nervous, I froze. 'But you must play on,' he said. 'The birds have already stopped to listen.' I was stupid and awkward, but I raised my eyes to meet his. I had to, of course; otherwise he would have been obliged to simply bow and walk away.

"My cousins were all over me. They could not believe what had happened. Did I intend to see him again? Well, we did meet again at the home of mutual friends. And Lady Wilde took a fancy to me. She wrote to me and told me how fond she was of me. I knew that something was in the air. Even my family were beginning to notice his attention. And then, just when I'd begun to hope, I had a note from him saying that he was off to America to subdue the savages, but that he would write. When the mail came each day, my heart would start its battering. I was terribly afraid that he would meet someone else."

"You were already in love."

"Passionately, but afraid he might not feel the same and I would die of disappointment. I was in Dublin when he returned. He'd scheduled a lecture about his adventures. We went, but I heard nothing he said. My head raced to its own design. My cousins suggested that we send up a note for him to join us for tea. Of course we had been writing, but you may know a thing in your heart and you're quivering and fearful that it won't come to pass. He called on me at my grandmother's house. I knew the moment I saw his face that my life was about to change. He'd had a ring made weeks before. All those fearful nights thinking he might have found someone else, and he had already chosen me."

She put a hand to her flushed cheek. "What they never understood about me was the depth of my passion. I had a quiet nature, but I remember the heat of him as he stood over me. He kissed my closed eyes. Beautiful grave eyes, he said. He saw through my eyes to my heart. He knew the truth about me. How often does anyone truly know you, Martin. This man understood passion and truth and nuance. He had looked into the heart of a flower and now he looked inside me

"But they would not even let me have this bit of happiness. My Aunt Emily, the one who managed my grandfather's house, thought me quite out of my mind. Marrying a bohemian? His life was too irregular. But grandfather liked him. They had lovely talks together. And the rest of Dublin, they thought me brilliantly lucky. I wrote to Otho. He *had* to take my part against the cold and practical Lloyds. I would die if I could not have this marriage. Otho has always saved me from despair. And so, we were engaged."

"And you never thought to ask about his ... irregular life? His bohemian ways?"

"He confessed to me that there had been other women and told me about his ... condition. And that he had been cured. I forgave him with all my heart. I told him that once we were married, I would hold him fast with chains of my love." Now she turned away from me and closed her eyes, put her fist to her breast and held it there in an undeniable gesture of self-accusation. "I have not done that. Instead of holding him fast, I have sent him to hell."

"Have you done that? You haven't yet convinced me, but we'll see." I walked to the door and called for Lady Brooke. "Your housekeeper can draw her bath now. She'll want a good breakfast and then we'll begin again."

She lay back, between worlds, her thick wild hair in disarray, her eyes bewildered, no, questioning would be the better word. Trying to make sense of what had happened. I kissed the backs of her hands, warm now. She held onto mine for a moment, her eyes soft with trust. A significant moment, and then the maid came in with her robe.

I left my patient to be helped out of a death bed into a warm reviving bath.

And I borrowed Lady Brooke's cabriolet and driver and set out to see the village doctor who had assured her that he could cure her with a *simple* surgery to the spine.

12

CHAPTER

English .....*Inglese*
Woman ... *donna*
Anger .....*collera, furore*
Scoundrel ...*scellerato, melvagio, mescalzone*
Dishonorable ...*disonorevole, vergagneso*
Surgeon ...*chirugo*
Unconscious ...*inconscio, inconsciente*

This ought to be vocabulary enough for me to make my point with the local butcher.

His name was Baldonado. He was short with a belly that pushed against his waistcoat, oily skin, a large pock-marked nose, and a few strands of greasy hair that had been combed across his balding head. He mopped at his sweated brow. "My dear colleague, you come under wrong assumptions. My patient suffered a blow to the spine. A piece of bone is pressing on the nerve. Unless the bone is removed, she will live in constant pain, suffer more paralysis and an early death. I assure you, no therapy of the mind will change simple physical facts."

"But you've felt that little piece of bone? You have physical evidence that the little broken bone exists?"

"What else could have caused these dramatic symptoms?"

"Have you ever heard of hysterical paralysis?"

"Only in English women. Here in Italy, no one gets paralyzed from hysteria. A woman has an anger, she does not hold it inside. She expresses herself."

"Under extreme circumstances. Something hidden in the unconscious."

"Italian women don't have an unconscious. Everything comes out. They scream, they cry, they pull their hair, they adore their children with a million kisses. If their husbands misbehave, they have a hundred ways of punishment. English women may be paralyzed by fear but not this woman. And my dear young colleague, please not to upset her before a surgery. She must be in a calm state of mind."

"Then you believe that her state of mind can affect her physical condition. You know that this woman has been under a severe emotional strain."

"And whose fault is that? Who but crazy Englishmen would have put Wilde through that stupid trial."

"Then you know who she is."

"A genius, that man. I have all his books."

"Then you can appreciate how the shock has affected her health. I don't mean just the trial. I mean a gentle-woman finding out that the husband she's loved and supported has succumbed to a terrible perversion."

"What are you talking about? You think she didn't know? Men of that type, especially in the theater, they make arranged marriages. A nice wife, a nice family and in private they indulge in their vice."

"You're not implying that a woman like Mrs. Wilde would have married him had she known!"

"Of course she knew. Women know these things."

"And you've told her what you believe?"

He wiped his sweating face with his rumpled handkerchief. "Told her? Of course I don't tell her. Women are fragile creatures. We love them, we bring them little presents, we cuddle them and warm them in bed. What this woman knows and what she says she knows, that my dear young man are two different things. We here in Italy, we know about women. Once she is on her feet again, she will find other men. Or she will go back to him. For his sake I hope so. Women are more resourceful than you think."

In that, he may have been right. "Where did you learn such good English?"

He offered me a cigar. "This is civilization, my young friend. Unlike your cold country, a civilization with a heart."

To be frank, in spite of myself, I found the man amusing. And then I saw something that sent a chill down my spine. Hanging on a hook in the door was his coat. Not just a frock coat but a coat covered with fresh blood and caked with old blood. The man was a primitive. This was 1898. Any good city surgeon worth his salt wore a white apron and operated in a scrubbed and disinfected operating room. But the old ones, the stubborn ones, they still wore what they had been wearing for a hundred years, an old blood-stained frock coat.

"Do you use strong anesthetic when you do spinal surgery?"

"Of course I use strong anesthetic. Do you think I am a barbarian?"

"Have you done this procedure often?"

"My dear young man, last year I operated on a hunch-back and turned him into a cricket player."

"But how many patients do you lose?"

He opened his pocket watch and snapped it shut. "What we save and what we lose are in the hands of God. Without the surgery she will not survive. And you intend to cure a patient suffering from creeping paralysis by hypnotizing her and doing hocus-pocus? No wonder your patients are hysterical."

A nursing sister came to tell him that he was expected in surgery. I was dismissed.

13
CHAPTER

Can't you forgive me for tonight? I will work hard and try to Improve. Don't be cruel to me because I love you better than anything in the world. After all it is only once that I have not pleased you. But you are quite right, Dorian. I should have shown myself more of an artist.... Oh don't leave me, don't leave me!" She crouched on the floor like a wounded thing, and Dorian Gray, with his beautiful eyes, looked down at her, his chiselled lips curled in exquisite disdain. There is always something ridiculous in the emotions of people whom one has ceased to love. .... " I am going," he said at last , in his calm, clear voice. "I don't wish to be unkind, but you have disappointed me.

Oscar Wilde, *The Picture of Dorian Gray*

I was not surprised to find her sitting up in a chair, wearing a robe, her hair brushed and combed back and tied with a ribbon. From the breakfast tray, she had taken some tea and toast; the rest she'd pushed away. As she leaned toward me, a spasm of pain gripped her. She took a deep breath to recover. "You *promise* me that you will find a way to help me make amends."

"When we understand the nature of the crime."

"... but you *do* understand the nature of my love?"

"... like the northern star, ever fixed in the firmament."

"The northern star? Martin, you know Keats!"

"Not at all. But you adore Keats. I saw this book at your bedside table in Tite Street and I see the book here. It was one of the precious possessions you salvaged that terrible day when the vultures descended. While you were in your bath, I thought I'd best read a poem or two."

"You and your passion for truth. You could have said, since you adore Keats how could I do less than read him too?"

"A lie is a lie. Even a lie that one tells to oneself."

"I haven't the energy to work out your cryptic remarks. And I would assume that you don't believe that love is like the northern star."

"Love is like ... a comet's tail, whizzing after the celestial body in great excitement, and as the comet dies, the tail goes off into bits and pieces to make new whatever it is that comet's tails make. I'm not good at these literary analogies. The point is that you loved Wilde immoderately. And so you saw nothing odd in your fiancé's behavior. You certainly saw the caricatures they drew of him."

"That was his pose, Martin, his stage presence. I am saying that I adored this man. I was madly and passionately in love and he with me. He wrote to all his friends about me, even to Lily Langtry. The first time she came to tea, I took her upstairs to show her my drawing room and she stopped me on the stairs. 'Do you know what Oscar calls you? His beautiful little Artemis. I can quite see that.' From Langtry herself."

"Pardon, I'm a clod with mythology. Who is Artemis."

"Bow and Arrow. Artemis, the hunter."

"Yes, slender ... and boy-like."

"Slender, not masculine. I see what you are digging for."

"I dig the way an archeologist digs. Go on. You were a woman in love."

"He telegraphed twice a day, he was so much in love. He told me he used to hand in his messages sternly, as if 'love' were a cryptogram for 'buy Grand Trunks' and 'darling' a cypher for 'sell on par.' He only wanted to please me. There was to be an engagement party. You had to see my aunt's face. An engagement party for an unchaperoned girl given by wild bohemians? She wouldn't permit it. I wept, I pleaded. Things happened, she said. Promises broken, a reputation compromised. Finally Otho stepped in and chaperoned me himself. Martin, you see how much I needed this marriage. For the first time in my life to have my freedom, and to be loved. I had my hand read. The stars were with me. I was destined to give myself body and soul."

"You believe in the stars."

"The stars reflect our destiny."

"And what star reflected that your destiny was to end up lying in a sick bed crying yourself to oblivion?"

"Your little editorial comments have barbs on them. I don't like them."

"If I were you, I wouldn't like them either. But we are in different positions here. I am the surgeon, probing for the bullet, so to speak, buried deep in the unconscious mind."

"You are a dear man, but you overdo the metaphor."

"Which proves what a good friend you are. Too honest to make social lies. We were speaking of the wedding."

"We decided to keep the ceremony small, just family and a few intimate friends. Of course all of London crowded outside St. James. It was him they wanted to see, but they were curious about me. If you could see me as I was then, not the wreck I am now. The dress was a creamy satin, low in the front, cut with a Medici collar, but I suppose you wouldn't know a Medici collar from an appendix."

"How well you know me."

"The sleeves were gathered, but the skirt hung very plain and Oscar had designed a wonderful silver girdle to gather it in. And my veil, saffron Indian gauze with pearls, and myrtle leaves in my hair. I thought of the many times my mother had criticized me. I never defied her. I simply cried. Now the Lloyds could watch me walk down the aisle on the arm of a man whose presence was coveted by every hostess in London and if my mother saw nothing but an awkward girl who wore the wrong clothes and said the wrong things, now she saw a woman loved, a woman who had the courage to wear myrtle leaves in her hair.

"My husband lifted the veil. The old life was gone and the new life began. We were to honeymoon in Paris. I remember standing at the rail of the ship, wind in my hair, blowing my cape, and my husband's arm tight around me. Safe. Finally safe.

"He'd chosen a charming hotel overlooking the Tuileries. He registered: Mr. and Mrs. Oscar Wilde. And we entered the room and closed the door behind us."

She put a hand to her pale cheek, suddenly colored by a flush perhaps of embarrassment. "If I had trembled at meeting him, imagine how I felt then. I've a small figure, he is a large man, great shoulders, strong hands. But gentle as I knew he would be. All I knew of the wedding night I knew from novels and the whispered stories of intimate friends. Martin, can I be utterly frank in describing this? Because if you want to know the woman who married that man, you must understand what that night meant to me. Nothing had passed between us but a kiss. Now he sat watching me as I began to take down my hair. He stopped me. He put his face to my hair and breathed it in, and with gentle fingers he took out the pins. It was my husband who unbound me.

More than my stays. He unbound my spirit. Think of what it means to a woman, the first touch of her husband's hand to her naked breast.

"The next morning as I lay languid in bed, he went directly to a flower shop and sent me baskets of flowers. I have never been so gloriously happy. We flew about on the wings of doves. We devoured each other at the dinner table. We met with his friends. We went to see Bernhardt, and after the play he introduced me as his wife. Wife. The sound of that word thrilled me.

"We returned to England on clouds of joy, in spite of the fact that his brother Willy had promised to find us a place to stay and did not. One could never count on that man. We went back to grandfather's and hinted that we would like to stay a while. But Aunt Emily never approved of Oscar and wasn't about to help the marriage along. But we'd leased a place in Chelsea and they'd given me five thousand of my inheritance. It would take months to redecorate and so we went back to Oscar's old bachelor rooms.

"But think of it, Martin, desperately in love and the whole of life ahead of us. Imagine what it meant to me. A home of my own. I can close my eyes at this moment and see it.

"You come in off the gray stones of the street to white woodwork and yellow walls. You walk to the back of the house, where light streams from the garden, and white carpet, and white lacquered chairs. No ponderous dining room table where guests pushed and clustered to take their teacakes. We'd built a serving shelf the length of the room. No one in London had it. And my drawing room. I can feel the balustrade against my hand as I walk upstairs. There my piano, and look up, at the ceiling! Peacock feathers! And at the back of the house, take a deep breath, you can smell it. Oscar's dark and mysterious smoking room with its divans and Moorish hangings. We had covered the window with Cairo woodwork to keep out the ugliness of Paradise Walk. The house backed up to that awful slum and every night there was a terrible racket, and after the children came, when they grew old enough to hear it, they used to think that devils and horrid creatures might climb up the back of the house to get them. I still dream of it sometimes, a lonely street with voices crying out of the fog and an eerie wind blowing leaves along a cold sidewalk, and I see a shred of torn veil ..."

"Have you had that dream often?"

"Yes."

"But you were safe and happy, in your own home at last."

"For a few months at least."

"A few months and you observed something ... unusual in your husband's manner and suddenly you understood that you had married a man with a dark side to his nature."

"A few months with a husband who was an ardent lover and I was pregnant. Ah, you missed that. You thought I had discovered something ominous."

I closed my notebook. "Rest for a bit."

She tried to push herself up from the chair and let out a gasp of pain. I supported her to the bed. "I surprised you," she said. "With the pregnancy."

"Yes I think you did."

She smiled. "Men are so sure of themselves. Let me hear you admit you were mistaken."

"I was mistaken."

"Then in some things you might be wrong."

"In some things I might be wrong ... but not often."

"... but you understand now what my husband meant to me. He had entered into my soul, and now I as carrying his child."

I drew the covers up about her. "Constance, I would have to be deaf and blind not to see how much he meant to you. I do understand."

"Yes," she said, "I think you do."

I kissed her forehead and left her. But glanced back as I was leaving the room. She had twisted in the bed to see herself in the mirror. She twisted without pain.

Margaret Brooke had tea waiting for me. I ate a cucumber sandwich and made notes while words were still fresh in my mind. She was smoking one of those blasted cigarettes. "You know that smoking is not only unattractive but ruinous to your teeth and lungs."

"Oh? Are you now my doctor too?"

I stopped writing." Her early years in that house meant so much to her. Do you remember it that way?"

"Her house? That place in Chelsea? It was his house. He chose it because his friends lived on that street. He designed the house. He furnished it. What did she have to do with it. I won't deny it was the place to go, if you were part of that crowd, but out of curiosity, and to listen to him, of course. He was mesmerizing."

I capped my pen. "I think she was simply going back to happier times."

"And when were those happier times? Ask yourself, why did he marry her. He could have had any number of women. He was clever; he was all the rage. She didn't have a fortune but she had enough to pay the bills so that he could write. To have married a wealthier woman would have been too obvious. And his mother fancied her. He not only wished to write, he wanted to change the London style. House Beautiful was what he preached. And he wanted the 'new woman' to be in it, at his side. They were to be the 'aesthetic couple.' He even dressed her for the part. I came to one of their literary teas. Women, the most beautiful in London, with their elegant hair and their jewels and their bosoms corseted in rich brocades, and she walks into the room as he designed her, in simple muslin, uncorseted, the natural line, he said, and her hair, a coronet braided with goose girl's ribbons. All eyes were on her, she on his arm as he led her into the room. This great bear of a man with his thick lips and his lachrymose eyes and his *trés* elegant clothes. And she? Drimp and drab, at least as he dressed her. I adore Constance but she hadn't the *élan* to carry it off. She looked like a failed scene from a play. You had to see the dismay in her eyes, and the clever little smiles of the handsome women around her. I thought she would faint. Are those the happy times she remembers? What else has she told you?"

No answer forthcoming. She snubbed out the cigarette. "I have put your things in the room next to hers. So that you can be close by if she needs you in the night."

14
CHAPTER

...might have been a Roosian,
A French, or Turk, or Proosian,
Or perhaps Itali-an!
But in spite of all temptations,
To belong to other nations,
He remains an Englishman!

Gilbert and Sullivan, *H.M.S Pinafore*

Satiric perhaps, but there is some truth in it.

I walked down the soft tree-lined road into the village. Damned fine weather. Feeling good. Was I smiling? Locals waved. Dogs came tail-wagging to trot alongside. I crossed a wooden bridge over a musical stream. The birds were in good voice. An excellent soft place while she was coming out of the shock of that ruinous marriage. But once the pain subsided, and it would, I had already seen the first signs, where should I take her for recovery? Not back to England where the scandal was still fresh and bloody. Perhaps Switzerland where she had a brother. I hoped to meet the brother who had so valiantly protected her.

I stopped at a small cafe, checkered cloth, flowers on the tables, mustached waiters. I wanted a good slice off a joint of meat but I had forgotten to take my Baedeker and so with gestures and "pidgin" English, I ended up with a meaty bone but with an excellent sauce. I finished with cakes, fruit, and a good strong coffee.

"I say, Frame!"

Across the room, two men obviously English, one waved, half- stood and gestured. Now he came toward me. Familiar, but from where?

He held a hand out to me. "Frank Harris. A friend of Oscar's? Don't you remember me from Astracan's party?"

The smarmy type who had provoked me. Damned if I would accept his hand.

"We've been to see Oscar and came down to speak with his wife, but she was too ill to receive us."

"As I recall, you were damned insulting about her when we last met."

He had the audacity to take a chair uninvited. "I was drunk. Can't actually remember what I said. But since the circumstances are so bad for both of them, can we call off the feud?" He waved for the waiter, ordered a bottle of wine. "Did you hear that Douglas had left him? He's in a terrible state. We came down here to prevail on Constance to meet with him. Sorry to find she's so ill. Then we heard that the English doctor had come to help her; doctor of the brain, they said. I had no idea you had a specialty of that magnitude."

"Abortioner was what you called me the last time we met."

"I said that I was bloody drunk that day. And you were hanging about her."

"If she's ill, it's because of Wilde and you have the gall to urge her to see him? Have you considered the affect on her?"

"Frame, he can't survive without some help from her. You know what that means?"

"It means that if a man is clever enough to write some humorous dialogue, he is entitled to be a self-centered bastard. What if he had been an architect or a brilliant mathematician? Would that still excuse him from decent behavior?"

"Have you ever read his books? His essays? Does it matter how he spends his nights? And those boys were renters. That's their livelihood. And none of us knew. It came as much of a surprise to us when we heard all that bosh at the trial."

"You didn't know he was a homosexual?"

"Not a clue."

"But Robbie Ross. Isn't he?"

"Of course Robbie, but Oscar was married. He was rooted with her. As long as he lived with her, there was a life for him. Get her on her feet, for God's sake. You don't know what we would lose with Oscar."

"Bugger off," I said.

"You mean you never cared about him? It was her you wanted? I can't see it. She's almost forty. In ten years she'll be a matron with a big bosom and you'll be in your prime. What is in this for you? You have money of your own. What in God's name do you want with the woman if not for Oscar's sake?" His friend was gesturing for him to leave. He put an unwelcome hand to my arm. "He never meant to hurt her, you know that. He was always very fond of his wife. If you knew Oscar, you'd know that he's a gentle sort. He would never intentionally hurt anyone."

"Odd then the damage he's done, not only to her but to his children."

He had no answer to that. He and his friend left. And I finished my coffee in leisure, watching the other diners, heavy men with big bellies, huge plates of food, bread broken off the loaf and eaten by being dipped in the red sauce which seemed to accompany most of the dishes. The women reminded me of Constance's description of the cabbage roses: big, velvety, luscious but going to seed.

I walked back in good spirits. I had taken a great deal of wine which left me, if anything, euphoric. Harris had asked me, what was it I wanted from this woman. What did I want, I thought, as I walked down this fragrant soft road listening to the lingering sound of laughter, the happy barking of a dog, a night bird's pretty tune. I knew what I wanted. I was not only Sherlock Holmes, I was Pygmalion. I wanted Wilde's wife walking happily and briskly beside me, knowing that I was the one who had brought her back to life.

I fell asleep that night in a feather bed, too soft for good health, but the windows were open to the garden, the night was seductive, and the promise of the next day's archeological dig was more seductive yet.

15

CHAPTER

The patient surprised me with the statement that she knew why the pains radiated from that definite location on the right thigh. The exact place where her father's leg rested every morning while she changed the bandages of his swollen leg. She did not think of the connection until today ... the patient as a rule was free of pain when we began our work, but as soon as I evoked some recollection, she reported some pain ...

S. Freud

This is not my concept of the "unconscious." To me the "unconscious" is a hidden motive underlying a course of action which the subject deems necessary for her survival. This hidden motive impedes healthy growth, and the challenge is to discover that hidden motive and translate it to her "consciousness." The key is logic.

"Four months of heaven, Martin, and soon I'd be beastly ill in the mornings and my skin would be dreadful. And the house was becoming terribly expensive. There were servants to be engaged and the upstairs made into a nursery. But I had a home of my own!"

"And that was important to you."

"Important? It was everything. If only fate had given us a little more time, shall I say, for romance? But doing the house was a great excitement, and when it was finished and they began to come ..."

"They?"

"Writers, actors, philosophers ... you have only to see my guest book. Of course that ended my dreams of going on the stage."

"Had you wanted to go on the stage?"

"For a brief giddy moment. And then I thought I might be a writer. I had some skill at it. When my husband became editor at *Woman's World,* he invited me to do an article."

"On what subject?"

"Muffs."

"Muffs?"

"There is a tone to your voice, Martin."

"Never intended. I am enormously impressed."

"And the book, of course."

"I had no idea that you'd done a book. Under what name? One of those fashionable *nom de plumes?*"

"Nothing tremendously brilliant. Some little children's stories." She sipped at her teacup and set it down. "Under his name. Mrs. Oscar Wilde."

"But why didn't you choose to write under your own?"

"Because I had no name."

" What was wrong with Constance Wilde?"

"I mean a clever name like those women he knew. The great Sarah or Sphinx or ... well they had such delightful little names. But mine was better. I was Mrs. Oscar. I was mistress of his house, soon to be mother of his child, and that was something to me."

"And your husband, he was satisfied to have this child."

"Ecstatic. Cyril was so beautiful a child, his father forever hanging over him, marveling at his little fingers. And when the baby cried, Oscar would pronounce, 'Positively Wagnerian. My son,' he kept saying, as if it were a miracle. 'My son.'"

"And so he was a good husband and father."

"A wonderful father. No better." She paused, a significant pause, a pause of omission.

"But?"

"But my days were so filled with the baby and he was so much in demand ..."

"... and?"

"... and by the evening I was exhausted, and sometimes .... sometimes he had to accept invitations without me."

The honeymoon was over.

"Martin, I was stupid. You mentioned the sheath. I ought to have asked. I know he would have agreed, but it was in my head that men did not enjoy it. Cyril was only taking his first steps and I was pregnant again." She looked toward the window. "Vyvyan was born, and then one night, my husband came to me, his infection had returned; well you know that story."

"He left your bed and you never thought anything but that he was concerned for you."

"No."

"You believed him absolutely."

"Yes."

"And after he left your bed, something in your life dramatically changed."

"Martin, after he left my bed, something in *his* life dramatically changed."

"You've implied that before. You actually believe that was why he took a male lover?"

"All I know is that he was busy with his work, meeting

with other writers, dealing with actors, yet never, never once did he miss one of my at-homes. And he adored the children. When they were just toddling about, he would get down on his knees and carry them about on his back, like a great bear. He was everything to his children. The toys he brought them, a little milk wagon with real cans of milk and of course he had to fill them, and they went sloshing around until the maid absolutely forbade it. Milk on white carpet! He could have been away traveling, or mounting a new play. But when they were at home from school, he was always there to be with them. In their room at night, telling them stories, Cyril curled in his lap, Vyvyan beside them, leaning against his arm, listening. There was one story in particular they loved. About the sad carp that lived at the bottom of Corrib Llough, his father's country place. It would only come to the surface if one sang a certain song. I'm not terribly good at the Irish, but I remember my husband singing, *'Athá mé in mu codladh, agus ná dúishe mé.'* She sang in a sweet sad voice. "It meant, I am asleep, do not wake me. And the story of the selfish giant which Cyril loved so deeply, and I remember one night, I was standing outside the nursery door listening, and Cyril began to cry. 'My sweet child,' said Oscar, 'has the story moved you so much?' And he said, 'I am crying because you will leave now and make Momma unhappy.'"

"Something came between you and this brief happiness and Cyril recognized it."

"Yes."

"And that something was a handsome young man who drew away the affection that had nourished you."

"Douglas? Oh, I blame the beast now. But then? I've already told you, Martin, it was a friendship with a young man who adored him as students adore their teachers. He was quite a good poet, and Oscar encouraged him as he encouraged others. He brought Lord Douglas to the house one night, absolutely charming boy, handsome, clever. Of all the young poets who clustered about Oscar hoping for crumbs from the master, I liked Lord Douglas best. He came to dinner with us. I found his mother charming. The father, of course, was a brute. Lady Queensbury divorced him, and the children took her side. Bosie was her favorite. Boysie they used to call him as a child. He was that easy sort of likable boy. And always about the house. Oscar trying to work and Lord Douglas dragging him away to lunch. 'Bosie again?' he would say. Lord Douglas ought to have been taking his examinations, and should have been studying. Oscar wrote to his mother, telling her of her son's bad habits. My husband was distracted from his work, they quarreled and broke off the friendship and Lady Queensbury sent Bosie off to Egypt."

"You mean that at one point, your husband actually had the good sense to break it off."

"At first. Then came the letters and the telegrams. He could not bear to lose Oscar's friendship. Would Oscar forgive him and take him back. He even threatened suicide."

"A suicide over a broken friendship. What on earth did you think?"

"I was worried about Lord Douglas, of course. His older brother had been killed in a hunting accident, and it was hinted about that it may have been suicide. And Lord Douglas had a frightful temper."

"And you saw nothing ominous in this."

"I suppose I saw it simply as the Greek thing."

"What sort of Greek thing?"

"My husband believed in Platonic relationships, older men to younger. And he believed in deep and passionate friendships. And so when Lady Queensbury asked me to intercede ..."

"Asked *you.*"

"Bosie could twist her about his little finger. She asked; what could I do. I was fond of her. I know how odd it sounds, as I tell it now, but then I simply saw Bosie as a self-indulgent young man spoiled by his mother."

"If Douglas had been a woman, what would you have done then?"

"An affair? I would have divorced him."

"For an affair with a woman but not for an affair with a man?"

"Will you *listen* to me? You say you are listening but you don't *hear*, Martin. I was a woman married to a famous man whose life was occupied with his work. This was the shape of my marriage. Lady Wilde was married to a man with three illegitimate children, and she said, I am above the commonplace. That was the shape of her marriage. My friend Margaret is married to this boor who is the white rajah of some wretched country. He lives elsewhere, she lives here. That is the shape of her marriage. I believed that my husband had become re-infected and that he stayed away from my bed because of it. How much that must have tortured him. So the void was filled with these intense friendships. And when I complained of his absences, there was always a logical answer. He had a play in rehearsal. He'd taken a hotel and would I be kind enough to bring him his mail. Or he was abroad to finish a play and he would write to Cyril, *Please take care of darling Momma.* And then he was home and we were together again. My dear friend at Babbacombe Cliff invited us to use the house for a family holiday by the seashore. And then Bosie asked to come along with his tutor to study for his examinations."

"You had nothing to say about it?"

"What was there to say? Oscar was always gracious. They were most welcome. Cyril studied Latin in the nursery, Oscar wrote his play, Lord Douglas and his tutor studied for the Oxford exams. And then they all went down to the beach to romp, like five children being dreadfully silly, and I was the clucking mother hen. I wasn't needed and so I packed up and went to Florence."

"But you were hurt."

"Annoyed."

"Only annoyed."

"I don't know what I was. Those were difficult days. Oscar took a house at Cromer to finish his play, Lord

Douglas went down to keep him company and fell ill, and Oscar had to nurse him. I wrote to them, if I were needed, I would be happy to come down to nurse Lord Douglas. I was at Babbacombe Cliff having a wonderful time."

"Were you."

Tight lips, no answer. She ran a finger over the carved wood of the arm of her chair.

"And what had your brother to say of this? You implied that he was your protector."

"He thought it was simply fame. Constant attention and self-indulgence. Don't you see, if Otho had suspected a perversion, would he not have snatched me away? It was not perversion; it was simply absence. Those last three years, he thought Oscar had gone quite mad. It was almost a divorce, he said. Oscar went where he pleased when he pleased."

"Surely at some point you must have suspected intimacy between the two men."

"... perhaps, in the middle of the night as I lay alone, I would reach out for my husband and he wasn't there. One thinks all sorts of mad things in the middle of the night. But not the sort of intimacy you imply."

"And yet you forgave him in prison."

"Yes."

"You were reconciled."

"... in a manner of speaking."

"What manner? Were you reconciled or were you not?"

"We'd had some brief ... arguments, but in the end I knew that it was my duty as a wife ..."

".... duty? All this had to do with *duty?*"

"... more than that, I wanted to see him again. I felt that I was the only one who could save him."

"Save him. You said that once before. Save him from what? He was already lost."

"Save him from worse."

"Worse."

"Yes, I knew what he had done and I knew that only I could save him from *worse.*

"Then why didn't you meet him in Dieppe when he was released?"

"You *know* why! The pain in my legs was so intense. But he had his allowance. I saw to that."

"You sent him money?"

"I told you that. It was I who paid for his first meal after those terrible years."

"A dinner is one thing. You make him an allowance?"

"When I arranged for the separation, I knew that he would have a terrible time before he could work again, and so I made him a small allowance, enough to eat on and to pay for his rooms. That allowance began the day he was released from prison."

"You intended to meet him, but you were too ill. You wrote him that."

"I told him if he would only wait until I were stronger, he could come to me. I'd taken an apartment near Margaret at Nervi."

"But something happened."

"Yes ...*yes!* I told you that I'd done something terrible!"

"What could possibly have happened between Dieppe and Nervi?"

"He intended to come. I wanted him to come. But then they began their little campaign against me."

"Who?"

"My family. When the trial began, I had nowhere to go but back to them. What was I to do? And they started once more with their I-told-you-so's. Now he was coming out of prison and they only wanted me to divorce him. They didn't care a farthing for me, but it was their name, you see. To protect their name. I was ill. And all I heard from them was: You are mad to see him again! How can you let him back into your life!"

"But you resisted."

"It was my life, I could live it as I wished. He had suffered so much, he deserved to have shelter and his wife's affection until he could get onto his feet again."

"But you weren't *on your feet,* were you?"

"Don't be clever. I'm saying that they were at me as they had been at the first and I resisted; but then it came to the children."

"In what way, the children?"

"Cyril was a beautiful young boy, they said. How could I let a father with such inclinations have his children back again? It was a horrid and beastly accusation. It was like a poison they planted in my head. I knew they were wrong, but of course I had to see him first. At least to be certain of his intentions. Don't you see, Martin, that I had to see him first?"

"Of course I see. It was a sensible decision."

"Was it? " She began to wring her hands. "And so I sent my sons back to school."

"Yes, and then ..."

"Can't you *see* what I did? He'd suffered so long; he'd dreamed of them for so long; he yearned for them. Martin, any prisoner, even a bank robber, comes out of prison and there is his wife and there are his children to fling themselves into his arms! And I had taken away his children! He thought he would never see them again."

"And he went back to Douglas."

"At first I was shocked, and then furious that after those two long years, after the letters and the anguish, that one simple request, that he see me first without the children; how could I know that he would run back to that beast?"

"... and ..."

"I stopped his allowance."

"Rightly so. "

"And Douglas' mother stopped his allowance. They had nothing to live on. Douglas left him. He's come back to Paris."

"Ah, I see it all now."

Her eyes were quite desperate, those hands wringing and twisting. "He is in Paris, drunk most of the time, without money. He cannot write. He is in hell."

"Who tells you this?"

"His friends. You see now why I am to blame."

"That I have not yet seen."

"But you heard my story! You heard what happened!"

"No, not the true story."

She was dumbfounded.

"At least not the whole story. Some truths, some rationalizations, some self-deceptions, many omissions."

She glowered at me. She gripped the arms of her chair. "You dare ... after I have told you the most intimate story of my life ... how ... how can you call yourself a friend and say that to me!"

"Easily, as it's true."

"But I have told you all I know!"

"Actually, you've told me what you want me to know and still preserve the image of a sacrificing wife."

She was dumbstruck. And then her tone shifted. "How beastly. I should slap your face for that insult to me."

"Then by all means do."

"How could you say a wretched thing like that to me? You made me believe I could trust you."

"My dear woman, I am the only one you can trust."

"To insult me that way!"

"Insult you? No, I would insult you if I let you get away with this casual recounting of events as the story itself. Do you remember when we first met? You begged me for the truth. Here is the truth. You have not even begun to tell the true story of this marriage." She twisted to turn away from me. "Listen to me. *Listen.* In the old days, when my father began his practice, a woman would never disrobe in a doctor's office. She would stand before the doctor, her face averted, he would get down onto his knees and reach up under her skirts to make his diagnosis. A woman would never consider taking down her drawers, even if it meant saving her life. You think you can tell me this superficial story, this rationalization, and think I can make a cure? If you want this to happen, you must take down your mental drawers. Bare yourself in all your naked feelings. And then ... then perhaps we can find out whether you really destroyed your husband or if indeed it is the other way around."

Distraught, she pushed herself up out of the chair and made her way haltingly toward the bed. I think her handkerchief was there. "How could you call yourself a friend?" She found the handkerchief, held it to her brow. "You are the liar." I moved quickly behind her to guard her from falling. "Cruel." She turned her shoulder angrily away as if to touch me was odious. "Unfeeling." And then in a burst of anger she whipped about and slapped my face.

I caught her hand and kissed it. I think she was shocked at the gesture and at my obvious satisfaction. She fell heavily to the bed, lay back bewildered.

Margaret Brooke, who undoubtedly had been listening behind the door, met me as I was about to leave for the village. "You do take risks, doctor."

"Living is a risk, Madame. Daring to live happily is the greatest risk of all. And would you wish me to take fewer risks and put her back into that dark room praying to her dead grandmother?"

A narrowing of the eyes, a deep probing search as if concentration could reach the inside of my brain. "We women, we use whatever armor we have to protect ourselves. You are tampering with that. Be careful."

She held the door open and closed it behind me.

16
CHAPTER

Mrs. Arbuthnot: You are right. We women live by our emotions and for them. By our passions, and for them, if you will. I have two passions ... my love for him and my hate for you ...do you think that terrible? Well, it is terrible. All love is terrible. All love is tragedy. I loved you once ... oh what a tragedy for a woman to have loved you.

Oscar Wilde, *A Woman of No Importance*

I entered that room to find an angry woman, hair tightly braided and arranged, robe of some dark mottled material, her violet eyes dark, very dark. "What," she asked, in a tone that was new to me, clipped, crisp and armed, "...what is it you write in that little notebook of yours."

I held it up to her. "This morning I was listing your strengths."

"Strengths. Is that an irony?"

"Not at all." I read from my book. " Strong enough to leave her mother's house. Strong enough to reject the wrong suitors. Strong enough to choose the most conspicuous man in London for a husband. Strong enough to wear trousers and preach sensible dress."

The rigid armor softened. "Ah, you heard of my famous trousers."

"I see you as a very strong woman."

Her shoulders relaxed. "I don't feel strong."

"Trust me, you are. So then, tell me, on the afternoon that your husband dressed you as the shepherdess on a Grecian urn, how did you feel?"

"Margaret told you. She talks too much."

"... and so?"

"How? It was a bad style for me. But I understood his theory."

"Were you angry with him for humiliating you that way?"

"Angry? No, I may have been .... embarrassed. I hadn't his confidence to carry things off. But he came to my rescue and I went to my room and changed."

"Then let me ask you this. He left your bed when he became re-infected; he went out in search of this Greek thing, and you understood."

"I may not have understood then. I think I understand now."

"You fell in love with him because of his philosophy. His voice. And what more? You and he discussed the future and you had the same life plan?"

"His life was fixed. I had only to fit into it."

"And did you fit into it?"

"As best I could. I was not like the other women he knew. They glittered; they were actresses, clever and beautiful. He saw something different in me."

"And you loved being Mrs. Oscar."

"I was proud of it. Yes."

"And when he left you alone during those last three years, you were willing to be patient. You knew he would come to his senses."

"... so I believed."

"Were you never angry with him?"

"I wept. I told you that I was unhappy."

"... not wept, angry. Were you never angry that he left your bed? Because you never said angry, you said sad."

"Of course I was angry, I was often angry. I am only human."

"Ah, that's the point you see."

"What point?"

"The salient point of your story. Because a woman who has your sort of illness is angry only with herself. And repressing that anger, she is liable to see a distorted vision and that might well affect her decisions. Do you follow me."

"Then, clever doctor, you have outsmarted yourself. I haven't that illness because I was often angry. I was angry with him when he came down to breakfast at two in the afternoon after coming in at two in the morning."

"And you told him so."

"I may have done."

"So here is a different piece of the story. You weren't simply the long-suffering wife of a husband occupied with his work. He came in late after carousing and you were damn angry."

"... not angry ... annoyed."

"How often. More than once?"

"Perhaps more than once. What are you getting at?"

"Was there anything else that made you angry?"

Her eyes were wary. She knew that I had come after her, and she was watching for me. "And would that be a sign of health, to be angry?"

"It would have been a sign of health if, when he came in at two in the morning after leaving you alone, you had met him at the door like a country wife and ordered him to sleep in the barn."

"But I understood."

"I know that you understood. He was clever and idiosyncratic and such a genius that he was entitled to three years of free time while his wife languished at home."

"It was not that way. It was ... my husband was not like ordinary men."

"In the fact of his vice, you mean."

"No ... he just did not see the world in a practical way."

"And how didn't he see the world?"

"He could not understand how a house is run. How one must manage money, for instance."

"He behaved badly with money, is that what you're saying?

"In a way, yes. He loved life. He gulped it down. He invited his friends for expensive dinners. He loved the grand gesture."

"Even if it came out of the household budget."

"I told you. He spent money unwisely."

"How unwisely."

"For the carriage."

"What carriage?"

"He liked to have a carriage following him about in the event he needed it. It was wasteful."

"And you told him that."

"Of course I told him that."

"You scolded him about money when he came down to breakfast at two in the afternoon."

"Not scolded ... I did not say scolded. I may have mentioned." Eyes suddenly wide with alarm, she recoiled; her breath came fast. "You think I am like my mother!"

"Ah, I never said that."

"You implied it."

I moved my chair closer to hers, looked directly into her eyes. "No, *you* implied it."

She gasped, drew away from me. She away, I moving closer, like a little verbal ballet. "Constance, you were nothing like your mother. She was cruel; you are essentially loving. And you were right to mention to your husband that he spent money like a drunken sailor."

"I would never have put it that crudely."

"My words not yours. What of his work."

"His work. What do you mean, his work."

"You supported his work."

"Of course I supported his work."

"And the book. The scandalous book. The one about the artist. The one they called immoral at the trial."

She stretched back her shoulders, twisted her body as if she wanted to escape me. "I thought that he hurt himself deeply by writing that book. But he wrote so many other books that were well received."

"You understood the theme of that book. You approved."

"He didn't ask my approval."

"You approved of his other books; you disapproved of that one."

"We had a simple disagreement, that was all."

"Disagreed on what?"

"On the meaning of art."

"And that was a simple disagreement? Duels have been fought on that one. With what did you disagree?"

"Martin, what does literary theory have to do with my hurting my husband?"

"Tell me your theory and I'll answer your question."

"I believe in God. Is that what you are after?"

'What on earth has God to do with anything?"

"God has to do with everything. Are you an atheist?"

"Of course I'm an atheist. I don't believe in heavenly mysteries or hocus pocus."

"Have you ever attended a séance?"

"Are you serious?"

"Ah, then you do not know everything. You have never seen a table rise or heard voices come from the dead."

"Good Lord, have you?"

"I have studied with Madame Blavatsky. I have seen proof that God exists. I believe that there is an order to the universe and a perfect morality based on that order, and that works of art ought to follow a perfect morality or else they are false. Does that satisfy you?"

"That mystifies me. Defying conventions by marrying Wilde and defying society by wearing trousers out on the street, and you believe in a perfect morality."

"Rational dress and falling in love with a poet have nothing to do with belief in God."

"Did your husband believe in God?"

"He had odd ideas; I never understood them. I left those to his intellectual friends."

"This perfect morality ... you loved the aesthetic movement, yet you believed that art must follow a perfect morality."

"Or else it is a lie."

"What of this aesthetic artist, the one who draws the sexual illustrations. You know the one I mean."

"Aubrey."

"Beardsley. Did his art follow a perfect morality?"

"He illustrated the text. He was not to blame for it."

"And your husband was."

She squirmed, she twisted. "Not in the way you imply."

"And you disapproved of *Dorian Gray*."

"He was mistaken in writing it. What has this to do with my legs? What has this to do with anything?"

"Was he offended when you told him you disapproved of this particular work?"

"I'm not sure we spoke of it."

"Then let's turn back to something else. How did you feel when your husband left your bed?"

"I told you that already. Why suddenly are you tormenting me?"

"The knife of inquiry is a sharp scalpel. Uncovering your story is like uncovering layers of infection. We take off one layer and here is another. I probe because there is something more. Something you haven't said."

"Now you are a mind reader."

"Good Lord, I hope so or else I'm in the wrong profession. Why did he leave your bed?"

She hunched her shoulders, turned her head to the left and to the right, as if her neck pained her. "This is intolerable. I've had enough."

"No, you simply want to escape from the truth. That day at the Cadogan, do you remember? You said to me that your friends would not speak frankly. Do you want me to be one of those friends? To yes everything, knowing that something is seriously wrong? Stop protecting him and just say it. There was another reason he left your bed and you blame yourself for it. In the same way you think you may have driven him away by becoming a scold about money and disapproving of his work. Why did he leave your bed?"

Silence. I could hear the ticking of a clock in the hallway.

"He left you after the second pregnancy. What happened during that pregnancy?"

"I heard you. I'm not deaf."

"... and so?"

"My husband was a lover of beauty. I was his Artemis. He adored my perfect figure."

"... and you swelled."

"He ... found it difficult to look at me. After the first delivery, I could not quite get my figure back. And then to be pregnant again so soon ..."

"My dear girl, you thought that your figure was spoiled and that was why he left your bed."

She anchored herself to the arms of the chair. "I was only just married. I was his pale lily, his fragile creature, thickening in the middle. And I did understand ..."

"Did you? The way your mother understood that your father loved other women and lashed out in cruelty and anger? Or did you keep what you understood sheltered next to your pained heart because you are essentially a good and loving woman. This business of Douglas. He came to the house and made a pest of himself but your husband was flattered by his attention and of all the others you liked him best."

"You know that."

"But your husband broke with him and the boy's mother urged you to influence your husband and take him back."

"She was afraid for his sanity."

"And a bright woman like yourself ... how many languages do you speak?"

"Are you being sarcastic?"

"You knew the friendship was perilous, a young man whose mother pandered for him. Why did you bring them back together?"

In a voice drenched in defensive sarcasm: "Well, you are so clever, Martin. You tell me."

"I am clever and I will tell you. You blamed yourself for being a shrew like your mother. He left your bed, you blamed yourself for that. Now he brings home this handsome uncritical boy, an easy friendship with someone who idolized him. Now if he had brought home a beautiful young girl, you would have, by your own words, divorced him. But this boy was one of your set. And you convinced yourself it was part of this 'Greek thing.'"

She sank back into the chair, her eyes filled with horror. "Lies, all lies!"

"Are they lies?"

"You are not only a liar but you are mad!"

"One of us is mad, mad with anger and frustration and guilt. This boy pleased him but when the friendship took him from his work, he thought better of the arrangement; yet you agreed to bring them together. What could have been in your mind?"

"Nothing was in my mind! It was a gesture!"

"Was it? When he went to where was it ... Cromer and he was nursing Douglas, and you said you were having a good time elsewhere but you would come and nurse his friend ... were you being sarcastic?"

"What do you mean, sarcastic?"

"Let me ask it another way."

"Ask me? *Ask* me? What ... am I on trial?"

"Yes, your health is on trial, your sanity is on trial. You were intending to put yourself into the hands of that dreadful doctor who operates in a filthy frock coat. I want to know what happened in that head of yours to make you so eager to give away your life. What did you write to him when you said you would nurse his friend. Was it a simple gesture or was there something behind it?"

"You are a devil, Martin, do you know that? You want to see the ugliest part of my self. You think that God intended for us to bare our basest natures?"

"Why is human nature base? If you believe in a perfect morality, then you believe in a perfect code of behavior. Yet part of you accepted the bohemian way. So let's not play that game. He was in Cromer with his lover."

"I forbid you to call him that!"

"I apologize. With his bosom friend. What did you write?"

"I wrote that I was having a lovely time and I would probably never be lonely again."

"I see. Letting him know that he could not continue to hurt you ... tell me you never suspected a relationship with Douglas."

"I've told you ...not that way ..."

"Look, I know that you loved him and his good fortune for it. He left you alone, he spent the household money on frivolities and yet you were loyal to him. When he sued for libel, you rushed to his side even though he had literally deserted you for three years."

"... because I knew it was almost over!"

"When his name was gawked at in the newspapers by every shop girl in London, you forgave him, even knowing that he had carelessly hurt his children. The day I saw you at the Cadogan, you wanted him to run. You were ready to meet him in Dieppe then."

"... because I thought he'd come to his senses. He'd made a terrible mistake. He'd been misled by that beast Douglas. And now he knew who really loved him."

"By the time he reached Dieppe, two years later, your legs could not carry you there."

She stretched out her legs and began to move her toes and twist her ankles. But almost maliciously. "That would give you enormous pleasure, wouldn't it, if my legs began to work again. You would be so bloody proud of yourself."

"*Bloody* proud? Of course I'd be bloody proud. I remember something from Shakespeare. What was the line? We would rather hold onto the ills we are familiar with than travel into a dark unknown place we know not of."

"This isn't a literary soirée."

"But you know exactly what I mean."

Her eyes were venomous; her mouth twisted with words that would not come out. If they had, what she spewed would have scalded me. I knew I had touched a very deep place. "Your father was a runabout. Yet you seemed to justify it since your mother was unloving. And if you justified your father, you had to justify your husband."

Venomous, smoldering. "Tell me, *Doctor* Frame, did you love your father?"

"Love him? I detested him. I welcomed his death. I am able to say that without guilt and my legs are working admirably well."

"You can say that without compassion?"

"He didn't deserve compassion."

Her hands, palms up, implored me "But I do. Let it rest now. Leave me alone now. Leave me some shred of my dignity."

"A dignified woman walking on a cane, or worse? No. One quick stroke. Finish it. When you tore the school tags out of your son's school clothes, when you were forced to tear him from his father's name, you hated your husband for what he had done to you. And yet you were ready to shelter him. You asked one small thing, to see him alone, to see his eyes and make certain of his sincerity before you allowed him to see his children. And he refused you even that. Why on earth should you think that *you* destroyed *him?* Isn't it the other way around?"

She watched me, lips tight, clenching and unclenching the weak right hand.

"No, there was something more, something essential you needed from him and that was why you asked him to come to Nervi."

"He was my husband! I had sworn to love him in sickness and in health."

"Pneumonia is a sickness. God didn't bind you to a man who slept with telegraph boys. Wrong reason. What reason might have been so compelling that it excused everything?"

She put her palms over her eyes. "I don't know. *I don't know!*"

"Answer this. Your husband, by your statement, is a drunk who no longer writes. Does not write or cannot write?"

"He can. He *can!* He wrote a poem in prison, a poem so tender and compassionate, it makes one weep to read it. It has been published here in Europe. It may not earn him a shilling but he is still a poet."

"You feel that he still has his talent but that he is too shocked by circumstance to write."

"Yes!"

"And with your help, he can write again. All he needs is his constant wife."

"Yes!" She turned her head aside. I heard a weak, "No."

"One or the other."

She twisted; she writhed; she bent over her legs; she opened her mouth to catch air.

"You know what you wanted from your husband. It was not something for him; he deserved nothing from you. It was something for yourself."

Cat's eyes, narrowing, very cold, very hard. "What for myself?"

"But you know. You are clever enough to have figured it out by now. Think back to that day at the house on Tite Street. The vultures rushed in and ripped away the fabric of your life. Your hand-wrought coverlet. Your husband's manuscripts."

She had pulled herself up straight in the chair, eyes open wide, jaw slightly unhinged.

"Your children's toys. I was there, Constance. You had moments to take what you could. Did you take a pocketful of toy soldiers so precious to your sons?"

"That's madness. Who would think of children's toys at a moment like that!"

"Of course. You took your clothes and furs, and then you asked me to bring something else."

Silence but behind her eyes, something was working, like gears in a machine. Her breath came in a hiss, like a snake.

"Constance, what on earth did you ask me to take for you?"

"My letters. The blue box of letters."

"That was a second thought. You sent me back for them, but it was too late. Come, what did you ask me to take?"

Oh, she knew exactly.

"You sent me for the guest book. Why that, rather than a precious toy soldier, do you suppose?"

Now the eyes shifted and changed. She shook her head, no, as if something had got into it and she had to shake it out. No. *No!* With effort she pushed herself out of the chair and moved toward the bed, clutching at the bedpost for support.

"You weren't a writer; you weren't an actress; you had written one little children's book and you hadn't the courage to publish that under your own name. But as his

wife, you had name, prestige, and all the literati of Europe fighting for your invitations. You had an identity, and perhaps, just perhaps you were willing to sacrifice for that."
She had to escape me. She could not. She held the bedpost and moved toward the table. From the table to the chest, to the window.
"He writes nothing now. But he still might be resurrected with the help of his wife."
From the window back to the bedpost, anything to walk away from my words.
"You invited him to Nervi because you knew that if you nurtured him, you might still have what you needed. But you loved your children too much. You *had* to send them away until you knew. You could risk anything but not your children. You had to know if he loved you. And of course he did not, or when he heard of your illness, he would have said, This woman has suffered for me. I can surely wait a few days, a month, a little half a year ... wasn't that also from Shakespeare? And he could not wait a moment. He ran back to his lover, on your money. Dear God, does the sky have to fall on you?"
Her breath came hard and quick. "How could I ever have trusted you. I want you to leave, today, now. Pack your things and get out of here!"
"Yes, you need time to think. Sit in the garden, under the trees. The air will do you good. Shall we meet, say in an hour?"
She moved quickly to the bedside table where her Keats lay open. She picked it up and threw it at me.
"... and," I said, picking up her book, straightening the bent pages and handing it to her, "... notice that, for the last two or three minutes, you've been moving with relatively little pain. But don't overstrain your legs. Those muscles are still very weak. We'll begin massage in the morning. I'd say that a few weeks of mild exercise and we can try a short walk. I found a lovely meadow near a tranquil pond. We might picnic there."

I bowed and closed the door behind me.

Lady Brooke was hovering, her cigarette in one languid hand, the other holding her elbow in what seemed an attitude of benign approval. "You are a clever one." "You had better go in to her. She'll want a sympathetic ear to curse me for ever having crossed her threshold. Then I think she'll have a good cry and a long sleep."

And so I left the Ranee's villa and took myself on the long carriage ride back to Genoa for a tour of the city. I had worked hard, I needed recreation. I played no musical instrument like Sherlock Holmes, nor would I defile my body with noxious substances. But I would enjoy a good meal, a good bottle of wine and whatever diversion the Genovese had to offer.

That night, lying in my fine Italian feathered bed, soft moonlight through swaying trees playing dancing figures on my ceiling, I permitted myself a small fantasy. I stood on a lecture platform before an audience of greybeards: *This woman was caught in a triad of emotions: First , her need to protect her children. Those of you who, like myself, are Darwinian will recognize this basic element in the evolution of the female of the species. Second, her vow to love and obey her husband until death do them part. And third, the hidden clue, pardon me if I allude to my friend Sherlock Holmes ... the guest book. This woman had frozen herself into an untenable position. Hidden anguish and visible pain. And once she understood, she was able to open her mind to the true picture. How quick to respond; how available to suggestion. My dear colleagues, we have only to listen to women ...*

I saw a book in it. Not just a medical text, but perhaps something that women themselves could read. Only a damn pity my father was not alive to read it. Bastard. I fell asleep on that. I woke the next morning, buoyant and ready for what was required, because, as I expected, the woman I would meet this morning was neither the woman

I had known in London nor the woman I had met just two
days ago here in Genoa.

She was a woman newly born.

I had delivered her.

17

CHAPTER

… so let us say that the woman who is liberated from the prison of her physical impediment finds herself free? And unlike my patient has no means of her own. What can she do? She is bound to her husband for survival. And if he is the cause of her "visible pain?" What alternatives present themselves to her? She can become a milliner, take in sewing, become a governess, or she can take a position as a typewriter for an assurance company which now, in a monumental advance for women, provides the advantage of a separate stairway so that girls need not be harassed by men in passing. We must not only free their bodies and their spirits, we must find ways to help them survive!

This "new" woman, this handsome smiling woman who waved a hand to me from the dappled shade of the grape arbor, when had I seen her smile before? A woman in a bright peasant dress taking tea in the arbor, her chestnut hair loose about her shoulders, a blue shawl against the cool of the April morning. Here was a portrait I would hang in my gallery of memories. And if that was bad metaphor, let it be, so much was I pleased by the sight of her. She poured me a cup of tea. Her right hand still trembled a bit, but it was steady enough for her to offer me the cup.

"My dear Martin, can you forgive me for doubting you?"

"What on earth is there to forgive?"

"A scolding, carping woman."

"A miracle woman," I said.

"Here is another miracle. This morning I woke to bird-song. I cannot remember when the birds sang last. It was as if they'd been silenced and suddenly were permitted to sing again."

I would note in my book: *The patient, self-absorbed in guilt and pain, hears nothing but the anguish of her own heart. And now the birds sing.* "Tell me how you feel."

"... odd, as if I were floating."

"You've left one world, you've not yet entered another. You are floating." I pulled my chair close. "The legs? The hand?"

"Tingling, pins and needles, but not the numbness."

With relief of the psychic pain, the natural movement of the blood is no longer impeded.

"And the back."

"An ache, but nothing of the excruciating pain."

"Time will cure the ache, as it will cure the ache in the heart."

"And that metaphor I will accept whole *heart*edly. I am so happy, I am willing to play any game. Or fight any war, because I think it was a war."

"You've survived an emotional battle. Now your courage

lies in trying to rebuild a new life for yourself."

"And what new life do you see for me?"

"More than most women in your circumstances can hope for. You are still young, bright, handsome, two fine children, money of your own."

"You think that a woman can decide on a life and simply walk into it."

"With my help, yes."

"And the next step is what?"

"Now that your mind ... your *mind* understands that your legs can walk without pain, we begin to strengthen those muscles. Massage for a month or so. Short walks out in nature to revive your spirit. Good nourishing food. And why not bring your children home? I've thought so much of your older boy, how hurt he must be."

A flush of excitement colored her cheeks. "God *bless* you for that. I have thought of nothing but Cyril this morning. Do you remember what you said that day at the Cadagon? When I could not think what to tell him about his father? You said that one day his father would explain it to him. You were so sage, so wise. But how could I bring his children back to him when he was so ruined?"

"Exactly. Your legs wouldn't carry you."

"But now! All that is changed because you have made me see the truth of my life. I was no writer; I was no actress; I even failed to be an understanding wife to this ... oh, he is a genius, I know that. And when I tried to go to him, when he needed me, I was too ill. My body would not let me because he was Humpty Dumpty, all in pieces, and I had no way to put him together again. There was no hope for me as he was."

A breeze ruffled the thick grape leaves of the arbor, making a whispery sound above my head. "How do you mean, as he *was?*" I opened my notebook.

She reached across and closed it. "We don't need this now. You knew the answer all along. You have changed my life. See how much you have changed it." She rose, and walked unsteadily to the table, to the tree, and then back again and took her seat. "Life has opened to me like a flower, now that I know you have the power to change him as you have begun to change me." I was for the moment disoriented. "Change him ... do you mean your husband?" "Go to him and ask about his childhood, and his father who kept a second family. And his sister whose death broke his heart. " The ground shifted under me. "You expect me to treat your husband?" "You have only to listen to him as you listened to me." "You cannot seriously ..." "... you are the only one who can hold the mirror up to *him* and find out why he sank deeper and deeper into vice because he had no strong wife to understand his needs and provide for them in some other way. I am so filled with hope, Martin, so buoyed with excitement. Think what you have done for me already. What had I to live for before you came and wakened me? Life with him was impossible. Life without him in the wake of that terrible scandal was hopeless. I was trapped, caged, and you have opened locked doors. Like a magician, you have willed me alive. A few months of walks in the nourishing air, and your wonderful hands at massage, I will be strong enough to send for the children, and together we will go to Paris."

Damn me for a fool. "Surely you can't expect me to take you back to the husband who has almost destroyed you and your children?"

"It was not him, it was his illness; I see that now. And once you have brought him back to the real world, he and I can begin again. My brother said it: Ten years abroad and if he writes and publishes, little by little he will regain respect. People must forgive, and when they see him 'cured' of his addiction, for I see now what it is, like a opium addict in those filthy places, when he is recovered, we can return to England and my son can have his good name again."

Had I a moment to gather myself, I would have held my tongue. But I had been so seduced by what I stupidly thought was absolute success and taken off my guard by her unexpected request that I blurted out, "My dear woman, I can cure hysterical paralysis and female ailments caused by repression and entrapment. I cannot cure an inveterate bugger who seduces errand boys with gold cigarette lighters. What on earth are you thinking?"

A sharp inbreath and then an exhalation, as if I had knocked her in the stomach.

"A new life means being separate from him. I thought you understood that."

Now I heard clearly the shift in her tone from sympathetic to confrontational. "How can you know that unless you try."

"I don't particularly want to try. I have no use for self-indulgent husbands who deny their wives and children for their own selfish pleasures."

Shocked silence while this sank in. Damn me. I was too blunt. I made a mental note never to be blunt in that manner. But the hammer had already struck its blow.

"And exactly what sort of life did you see for me? Marriage to some solid lawyer or someone in trade who would agree to marry a divorcée of an infamous man? Or shall I end up like my two Russian countesses, going from *pension* to *pension*, living on dreams and drinking endless tea from an ancient samovar?"

"You? Never." I tried to take her hand. Pointedly she withdrew it. "You are just out of an illness, still weak. You can't know what sort of exciting life awaits you."

"Oh, do you think so? Perhaps some man so out of public life that he has never heard of my husband? Some provincial town where the ladies might suddenly come upon the truth and speak behind their hands. "Do you know who she is? The wife of ... poor thing .. how she must have suffered; oh my dear, do you think she actually knew?"

"Then make a life of your own, an independent woman. I can easily see you as a public figure helping other women like yourself."

"Helping how?"

"... how? When women learn how you have been cured by talk alone ..."

She was horrified. "Surely you did not intend for anyone to know about this!"

"... but I thought that certainly ..."

"... certainly what? What I revealed to you was confession between patient and priest! Surely you would never have repeated it to anyone!"

Damn me to hell for an idiot. "No, of course not but I thought ..."

"You thought what!"

"That you wanted to be of help to women. You fought for rational dress. You've spoken at political meetings ..."

"... and you thought I would get up on a platform to speak of this intensely personal...you couldn't have done!"

"No, certainly I didn't intend ..."

"Then what did you intend?"

"Constance, listen to me."

"Oh," she said very pointedly, "I am listening."

For the first time I was at a loss for words. I stammered, I hesitated.

She gripped the arms of her chair and leaned forward. "I understood this morning how much Oscar had used me. But he was a genius, you see. Audiences watched his plays and laughed until the tears ran. They read his book and fist fights broke out over his words. His children's stories made mothers weep. And he married a woman he could use, in order to survive a world that was never generous with him, not as he was. Yes, he used me. Can it be that you have also tried to use me? And who are you, Martin? I know who my husband is, but exactly who are you?"

I stammered, stumbled, dropped my notebook.

The next question came clear and without emotion. "My

husband is sitting in a cafe in Paris, drunk most of the time, without money most of the time, except what he can borrow from what are left of his friends. He has sunk so low that I cannot describe the kind of life he is leading. So, can you or can you not cure him so that I can return to him with his children?"

"I ..."

"A simple answer. Yes or no."

The answer wasn't simple. "No."

She closed her eyes.

"... you must understand ..."

"I understand quite well." She pushed herself out of the chair, made her way carefully toward the house, calling to the housekeeper.

Hell and damnation.

The housekeeper, black skirts flapping, came running. The little gnome, who looked at me with scolding eyes, helped her Signora back to the house. Now the Ranee came flying, still in her morning robe, her hair unpinned. "What has happened?"

"A bit of a setback, but not to worry. Just let me work it out."

"Setback of what sort?"

"That husband of hers. I had no idea the power he has over her."

"Ah, I could have predicted ."

"Let me think it through. I'll return in an hour. Look after her."

The cabriolet was at my disposal. I took it without the driver, whipped at the horse and set out for the village. Too fast, I almost overturned when a wheel hit a rock. The horse whinnied and snorted his displeasure. I reined up before a little bistro which was serving coffee and sweet cakes to men who sat with their morning newspapers. I took a quiet courtyard table and ordered a bottle of wine. Wilde was a devil. He had a grip on her I could not break. But in one thing she was right. How did I honestly expect to reveal this "cure?" What was I thinking? That I could actually write a paper? Even if I disguised her name, the circumstances would point her out. And without the circumstances, where were my brilliant results?

I wasn't Pygmalion. I was Icarus. And I had fallen.

I descended through several rungs of hell. By the time I consumed enough wine to ease the shock of my predicament, I was too drunk to get myself back into the carriage. Drunk enough so that one of the waiters put me into a back room and let me sleep. I awoke thick-tongued and heavy-headed and called for coffee. The proprietor himself brought me a cup of thick black stuff strong enough to eat the hide off a rhino.

Sickly sober, and with sobriety came anger. At her. I had showed her the road to sanity and she only wanted to jump back into the pit.

Next came cloying self-pity. I had come at my own expense. I had pulled her out of the lower depths literally overnight. And was she grateful? Her only concern was for that husband whose bloody selfishness and self-indulgence had caused her illness.

Finally, when I was totally and brutally sober, came the question more bitter than the muck that passed for Italian coffee.

Where did I get the idea that I could make instant cures?

To a point my theory was right. She was frozen by indecision. When she understood the nature of her dilemma, her muscles relaxed. But when she felt she had found a way back to the life which had once sustained her, she flowed with energy again. With her new energy, she had made a decision. Unfortunately her idea of decision was not mine. What now? Where did I go from this very sticky position?

She wanted me to cure Wilde. Could homosexuals be *cured?* Could men who fancied pretty boys be cured was a better question. And how to begin again since she now believed me to be self-serving.

And in a way that was true.

But self-serving only in the greater service of women.

What to do. I looked at my watch. Late afternoon. I had been gone for hours.

The cabriolet stood outside, the little horse snorting impatiently, pawing the ground to show his displeasure at my desertion. My head was splitting with migraine as we bumped along the road. What was my next move? And how was I to explain not only my absence but my deplorable condition, rumpled, wine-stained shirt, smelling like a brewery. In this ignoble state I returned to the Ranee's villa.

A frantic Ranee met me at the door. "Where have you been?"

"Trying to work through a viable plan." And what was my viable plan? A shot in the dark. I would play for time, using exercise and massage as an excuse; then if he was still what she wanted, I would agree to take her to Paris. But not yet; soon. Clearly manipulative, but it would give me time to make her see the light. "I'll just clean up before I see her."

"She isn't here, you fool. You ought to have stayed with her. She fell ill the moment you left. Unbearable pain in her back. She cried out in agony. She insisted on having the village doctor. He came and took her to the clinic."

Bloody hell. "Why did you let her go?"

"How could I stop her? He convinced her that you were a mesmerist. That a clever manipulator as he knew you were could convince her that the pain was gone when it was still present."

"But that's nonsense."

"How was I to know? I've heard of men in a hypnotic state lifting a heavy wagon. Martin, I warned you ..."

"Right. Save the recriminations until we bring her back."

"You have mucked things up."

"Just let me take her out of that medieval torture chamber and then call me what you will."

18
CHAPTER

Now I come to the third period of our treatment. The patient felt better. She was psychically unburdened and less restrained; but the pains were manifestly not removed; and reappeared from time to time with the old severity ... While working one day, at this time she was free from pain ... I heard the steps of a man in the other room. Now she changed, gait and mien, with the sudden appearance of violent pain.

S. Freud

How did I miss this.
I simply had not read it.

Try to speed down an Italian country road in a small cabriolet. We hit every stone, every rut, we were stopped by sheep, by hay carts, by a pebble in the horse's shoe. It was five in the evening before I reached the clinic. I ran up the steps and slammed the door knocker, which I noted in my anger was a grinning satyr. The door was opened by a nursing sister. "I am here to see Mrs. Wilde." Or did she call herself Holland? I began again. "I am here to see the English patient."

She answered something in Italian and shut the door in my face.

I knocked again, furiously. She opened the door. I stuck my boot in and stopped her. "Look here, I intend to see the English woman whatever your *dottore* may say, so just let me in."

She was flustered. She called to another sister, a tall big-bosomed woman with a face like yesterday's pudding. It was impossible, come back again, please to go away.

"Then I will see Dr. Baldonado."

She lapsed into Italian, making wide hand gestures of explanation, rushed down the corridor and stood defensively before a set of double doors. I pushed her aside and knocked. She came behind me and grabbed at my coat to hold me back.

I knocked harder. "Baldonado!"

I heard the lock on the door *snap* closed.

I slammed on the door. "Let me in or I will send for the gendarmes or whatever you call the police in this bloody country."

Click. He opened the lock. I pushed the door with such force that he fell back to the floor. I bent over him, clutching his collar. "Where is she? I'm taking her out of here, and now."

He gestured, he spoke in fast Italian, he shrugged his shoulders, he mopped his sweating face. "You were very wicked. What did you promise the poor woman? That she could walk again without surgery? I explained that it was impossible. That the bone was pressing on the nerve. It was only a small procedure."

"You intended to operate without letting me see her. Well then, I will cable her brother. Let him decide for her. Now get her dressed. I'm taking her home."

Drops of sweat rolled down his face and a wet circle spread under his armpits. "She was very anxious. She said that she had to go to Paris. She wanted the surgery as soon as possible."

"Do you mean today? You intended to operate today? Is she sedated? If I have to, I will take her away asleep."

He did not answer. And then I saw the blood stain on his sleeve. Not only on his sleeve. *He was wearing the bloodied frock coat.*

I felt heat rising to my face. "You couldn't have done. Not so quickly."

Great drops of perspiration ran down the side of his oily face. "The nursing sister was here to assist me. It was a small matter, just a little incision to take away the piece of bone. She understood. She insisted."

"You've gone and cut her? How is she? You didn't find the damned bone, did you. I'll personally wring your neck for the harm you've done."

He mopped at his brow. "Without the surgery she could have expected paralysis and death. She could not live with that terrible pain."

I took him by the collar and dragged him to his feet. "What happened! Show me what you've done to her!" He slapped at me with his pasty hands. "Show me!" He looked desperately at the door behind him.

The door led to a small operating theater, if you could call it that. Just a small white room with many lamps and a hanging lamp over the operating table which was a plain wooden table with a rubber cloth tacked around it. She lay sprawled on her stomach, covered with a sheet, her arms hanging limp at her sides, her bare feet exposed. A sick

spasm gripped my stomach as I realized that he had already
begun the surgery. She was anesthetized. On the sheet,
which covered her inert body, I saw a spreading circle of
blood. Not only on the sheet but blood seemed to be seeping from the wound and dripping to the floor. *He had
opened her and had not closed the wound!* Worse, on the
floor beside the table was a simple pitcher of water. *He had
cut her and was simply washing down the wound with
water!* Barbaric! He had begun the surgery, discovered no
small broken bone, and hearing me enter had simply left
her there. I would kill the bastard with my own two hands.
But not until I repaired the damage. I pulled off my coat
and rolled up my sleeves. I saw the bowl of soapy water
and scrubbed my hands. Thank God he had done that at
least. As I moved to the side of the table, I felt something
sticky under my shoes. Horrified, I realized that I was standing in her blood. As God was my witness, I would crucify
this bastard for what he had done. There would be an inter-
national incident of enormous proportions. I reached for
her hand to take her pulse. I had no idea how long he'd
had her under or what anesthetic he used. But the wound
had to be closed before the loss of blood caused a shock to
her heart. I pressed my finger to the artery. Wrong spot, I
felt again. My heart skipped and then began to pound.
There was no pulse. I felt at her throat. No heartbeat. *But
the hand was still warm!*

I screamed, "Baldonado!"

Two nursing Sisters pushed me away from the table and
covered her with a white sheet. The blood was still wet
enough to seep through. *She was still warm!* It had been
moments ... *moments!*

My memory of what happened next is flawed. I know
that I ran back to that filthy butchering bastard, dragged him
out of his chair and struck him with my fist. He screamed,
"You weakened her! She told me what you did. It was your
fault!" I struck him again. He went down. He shrieked for
the *polizia*. The Ranee came rushing in. "He's killed her," I

said. She and I ran back into that terrible blood-dripped room. I remember thinking ... this is the torture chamber of my child's nightmares. She lay on her back, now wrapped in that white sheet, white but stained with touches of blood. Her eyes were closed, her hair alive and vibrant framing her face which seemed simply relaxed in sleep. The Ranee cried out and slumped in a faint. Revived, she wept. I wept. The nursing sister asked us what priest to call, where was the funeral to be. I think it was only with the word "funeral" that I finally understood that she was dead.

"What shall I do?" wept the Ranee.

"You had best cable her brother."

"Ah, those poor children."

To my everlasting regret, I did not examine the body to see exactly how he had killed her. Cut a nerve in the spine? Kept her under too long? Was the offending bone there or not? But at that moment, she was not a "body." She was Constance, my patient and my friend, and she was dead.

They laid her out in one of the clinic rooms, curtains drawn, candles lit, many candles and vases of roses, those cabbage roses she had described to me. The sweet nauseating odor of rose permeated that room. Above the bed, looking piteously down on her, was a carved wooden madonna, a single tear falling on a painted wooden cheek.

I myself drove the Ranee to see the Protestant minister. They would bury her on a hillside outside Genoa. She arranged for the stone, an engraved leaf pattern. Constance Mary, daughter of Horace Lloyd, QC. and a verse from *Revelations.*

As if she had been a virgin, never married. Missing was the name Wilde.

The burial had to await the arrival of her brother. Both of us sick to the soul, the Ranee and I returned to her villa, closed the drapes, and sat in a darkened muted day room for our deep mourning and self-recriminations. The little housekeeper brought tea but dissolved in tears and, apron over her mouth, went shrieking from the room. The Ranee lay on a sofa, handkerchief over her eyes. "I should not have let her go, but the pain returned with such intensity."

"Did she say anything before she left?"

"Just that she wanted that awful doctor, that he was always sympathetic. When I begged her to wait for you, she said that she was putting herself in the hands of God, that only God listened. Martin, what happened. Did you argue? What had she said that upset you?"

"Less an argument than an inappropriate request. I had to think it over before I answered her."

"Something to do with her husband," said the Ranee.

"Always her husband."

"She would never let go of him."

"She had the mad idea that if I could cure her, I might cure him."

"The power of that sad marriage."

"She would have gone back to him. She asked me to take her to Paris."

The handkerchief came off the eyes. "She asked you *what?*"

"To take her to Paris. It was impossible of course. She was so tied to the man that even when she knew she could be cured, all she could think of doing was returning to that sad, damaging marriage."

"She *asked* you to take her to Paris and you hesitated? You fool!"

I was frankly shocked. "Fool? *I'm* the fool? You know that the man was hopelessly ruined."

"Of course he was ruined. Don't you understand? She would have taken one look at that fat drunken husband and run from him. She would have run on the arm of a handsome young man. Oh, you stupid idiot. You might have saved her."

"What the bloody hell are you implying?"

"Why do you think I invited you into my home?"

"Why? To bring her out of her pain and paralysis with a talking cure."

"That nonsense? I invited you to stay because she was

fond of you. She was a woman whose husband had left her bed. She was deeply wounded. I told her, the only way to survive is to throw your hat over the windmill. She only needed an affair with a man who loved her. She tried, she could not because of the force of that stupid marriage. And then she began to speak of her friend Martin, her dear Martin, her kind Martin. She only needed to be loved again."

"Loved?" I jumped up, overturned a table. "Loved by me? You thought I would ...are you mad? I happen to be a doctor, not a renter!"

She dabbed at her throat with her handkerchief. "And not very good at that either. She is dead, is she not?" She touched at her eyes. "The fault is mine. I seem to have sent a boy to do a man's work."

"And you Madame can go to bloody hell."

In a fury I threw my clothes into my travelling case. She stood over me. "I warn you," she said, "if you repeat what happened in these rooms to anyone, if you let loose one word of what she confided to you, if you tell anyone that she wanted to go back to him, I will tell them what the surgeon said. That you weakened her with your questioning and badgering so that her heart gave out. He blames you, and so do I."

I tossed my notebook into the case, closed it and shoved past her.

"As to Paris," she called out," ... on your head be it."

Bloody stupid woman. I started down the road on foot, hailed a ride to the train station. I rumbled along the road in a milk cart, feeling ill, sick at heart.

No train to Milan for an hour. I slumped on a bench, hot, feverish. When I closed my eyes, I saw images of her body on that torture table, felt the sensation of sticky blood beneath my feet. Why had she chosen death when she knew she could live? For love? She was fixed on this wreck of a man and love was like the northern star? It was a bloody poem, for Christ sake. Give me love or give me death, like Camille? Camille was a silly story. Take her to Switzerland, cure the lungs, let her go back and find a new lover. And she said that God listened and I did not? Speak to Him and see what He can do for paralysis and an aching back.

When the anger subsided, hot guilt washed over me. Had it ever crossed my mind to have an intimate relationship with the woman? Only in fantasy. She on the speaker's platform beside me, the two of us revolutionizing the treatment of women, and then traveling together, she was so passionate, I understood her so well, and some evening, in rooms side by side at the hotel, perhaps by accident ... but it was only a fantasy. I would never have acted on it!

At that moment my anger at Wilde was born. Blood pounded in my head. It was always Wilde and even at the end she could not bring herself to blame him. Well I blamed him. They had punished him for his indiscretions. But for what he had done to her, he had not yet paid. When I finished with Wilde, he would pay for his ultimate sin: his sin against a dead wife and two motherless children. I wept for her children.

The conductor called my train. I had only time to cable Robbie Ross. *Constance Wilde is dead. Where can I find Wilde? Cable Milan*

I boarded the train. A slamming of compartment doors, cries of the conductor, a hiss, a jerking movement. And so we chugged away from Genoa with its disordered gardens, where the cabbage rose opened her skirts too soon, went to seed and then to rot. Sick to my stomach with the rolling of the train, I fancied I smelled the rank odor of roses. I slept as if drugged. Woke, ordered tea, took little even of that, and slept again. When the train finally pulled into the Milan station, I made my way to the cable office. Ross's message was there. *Poor Constance. He is devastated and is begging me to come. Yes, by all means, comfort him. Will arrive in two days. He stays at the Hotel D'Alsace, Rue des Beaux Arts. Goes by the name of Sebastian Melmouth.*

Comfort him? That was not my intention.

I awaited the Paris train, shivering with cold. I had left

my greatcoat behind me in Genoa. I huddled on a bench, dropping off fitfully, jerking myself awake when I heard the Paris train called. I boarded the train in a high fever. I slept all of that journey. My anger at Wilde dissolved into fever dreams: *My father dragged me down into his surgery but the room was a cavern, water washing down the stone walls. But the water was red!* I woke with a cry, and slept again. *I was underground in a coffin, screaming, I am alive! Let me out!* The journey seemed interminable. I ate little, slept badly. The conductor shook me and told me we had arrived in Paris. I would have gone directly to Wilde's hotel but I was too ill. The porter had to help me to the boat train. I remember nothing of that crossing except that some kind woman fed me tea.

I arrived back in London half dead.

I spent the next three weeks in bed.

It was in these fever dreams that she came to me and would come again throughout the next months whenever that fever recurred. *I entered an operating theater and saw her strapped to a table but I was frozen, unable to move. She was awake, in pain, pleading for me to help her. The butcher stood over her, a knife in his hand. He touched the tip to her delicate skin. She screamed soundlessly. He drew the knife down. Ruby beads rolled down her back onto the rubber sheet that lay cold beneath her and puddled onto the floor.*

I awoke in a cold sweat.

It was late summer before I finally recovered enough to go back to work.

My experiments with the female psyche were over.

19
CHAPTER

My spirit is too weak; mortality
Weighs heavily on me, like unwilling sleep,
And each imagined pinnacle and steep
Of godlike hardship tells me I must die ...

Keats

It was Keats that ruined her. Bloody romance
that fogged the mirror of reality. What is wrong
with: I am the master of my fate; I am the captain
of my soul?

The Case of the Pederast's Wife

Not a word from Robbie Ross, who must have thought it odd that I never reached Paris, nor had I been in contact with him since my return. But he was too much a gentleman to inquire. Two or three times I sat down to write him a note, but I could not find the words. Images came rushing back, followed by a relapse of that dreadful fever which was God knew what sort of pernicious Italian malaise. In my fever dreams, she was always there, sitting in a chair near my bed, glowering at me; or standing in a corner, her eyes dark as coal, accusing me. And I woke with a cry, to find a pillow on the chair or a lamp standing in the corner.

I did not completely recover my strength that year, and between patients I would find myself sunk into a dark reverie, arguing with her, and shake myself out of it, heart pounding.

By year's end my health was still precarious. But my gentleman's obligation forced me to send around a note to Ross, inviting him to join me at dinner. I fortified myself with hard spirits in anticipation of a difficult evening. But he only greeted me with concern. He felt that I must have been indisposed. He worried about me and had asked mutual friends, learned that I had indeed been ill. He knew of my concern for Constance, and thought it enormously kind of me to have gone to Genoa to comfort her at the end. It was a tragedy the proportions of which had not yet been measured. Not only the impact on Oscar, but on the children.

"Will they now go to their father?"

"If only they could. But when she made the separation, he agreed that she should appoint a guardian for her sons. It was terrible for him, knowing how much her family detested him and he begged her to choose someone who would not separate him from his children completely. They settled on a cousin, a decent man, at least Oscar thought so. Nobody really wants the children. They were evidently told the terrible news of her death at school. That younger boy, at least he had the Jesuit priests who would break the news to him kindly. But Cyril. God knows how they told him. And no one in the family wants them." The waiter came, we ordered, Ross looked about to see that we were not overheard. "The children are an embarrassment to the family. They reek too much of their father."

"But surely Wilde can petition to see them."

"He has tried to write; but the guardian absolutely forbids any letters to be forwarded to the sons from the father. So you see how trapped he is."

"How did he take her death?"

"Very hard. He did love her, you know."

"Robbie, I'll tell you frankly that I don't know that. A man is known by his actions, not his intentions. Where do I see in his actions that he loved her? To love a woman is to protect her. And to me it was the other way around until she could no longer continue because of his ... his incomprehensible attachment to Douglas."

"Not knowing Oscar, I can quite see how you might think that. He was terribly fond of her. But you cannot understand the power of his passion for that rotter Douglas. It overcame his sense of obligation. I rushed to Paris after I'd cabled him about Constance. I found him in his room, weeping. I thought he would die of despair. He said, If only I could have seen her, if only I could have kissed her once."

"What prevented him from going to her when he knew she was so ill and kissing her then? It might have meant a great deal to her. I think with him it was always a question of her money."

Bread and butter were brought to the table. He broke a piece of the bread and crumbled it on the cloth. "You have to know Oscar. He is the kindest soul, but there is something about money which brings out the worst. He was devastated, and yet he complained to me that she had arranged the April payment before she died, his money comes in quarters, and that the next quarter ought to have come in advance; he had nothing to live on, and could I please find out when the money would arrive." Those words were a cool balm to my heart. The man was exactly as I had known him to be, selfish and egoistic to the end. "Is it true that except for her money, he is penniless?" "Close to it, and when he gets a gift of money he manages to squander it on pleasures. But what else has he? He begs from his friends. It seems that whatever was important to him, his art, love, his family, now it is only the money. He says he needs her allowance so that he can take two rooms, one for insomnia and one to write in. And then he says, Both for insomnia. See here, Frame ..." The look of petition in his eyes chilled me. Thankfully the dinner came, and he was put off until dessert. "What I wanted," he said over coffee, "what I wished to ask of you ... you were with her at the end. Did she speak of him in anger?"

"What makes you think that?"

"He had written to her just before she died, and she seemed no longer to welcome his letters. He cabled me in distress. *I think she wants me dead.* And then suddenly, just before the surgery, she wrote him a lovely letter. At least he has that. And I know he would be so much comforted if he knew that she didn't hold this terrible anger against him."

I fiddled with an apple tart, smothered it with rich cream which ordinarily for my health's sake I would not take. "Actually, she spoke most lovingly of her husband."

He took the liberty of putting his petitioner's hand to my arm. "Then go to Paris. Tell him. This business with his wife, it's a dagger in his heart."

I said that I would consider his request but this was a bad time for me. He quite understood. At least he politely said as much.

I went back to my work. I needed my work. I needed a new specialty And so I began to study, not the psychology but the physiology of the heart. With the new year I plunged myself into my practice, treating the women in my care with compassion, attentive always to the full scope not only of their symptoms but their problems with husbands, children, parents, taking care *not* to make suggestions as to any "unconscious" sources of their sour stomachs and their flatulence and their constipation and their back pains and the spots before their eyes and their fits of weeping. I became a concerned and affectionate listener, always careful to warm the stethoscope before I put it to a heaving breast. And in the evenings, I prepared myself for another life. I had it in my mind to get rid of my father's house, to leave London, or possibly to emigrate.

I was still troubled with occasional bouts of fever and those damned nightmares. In my dreams I walked down deserted streets, and suddenly the wind swept a bit of veil along the sidewalk, and I would see her standing near a wall and she would hold a hand out to me. Or I would be back in my mother's room and rush to her bed and she would turn toward me and I would see Constance's face. In waking hours, I might be rushing along the boulevard in a crowd, and I was sure I had seen her. Once I actually approached a woman in a restaurant. It chilled me to the bone to think that my mind was taking such a turn of the bizarre. My only true comfort that year was my little actress. "Martin, what on earth is *wrong* with you."

Alma Belmont was actually no longer a "little actress" taking understudy parts. She was the up and coming Alma who had taken her audiences by surprise when she understudied a musical show and was now the leading star. She gave up her other "gentlemen," staying solely with me. She was my comfort and my consolation and one night I simply told her the story.

She held me in her arms and wept.

I had lost something in myself, I said to her. I needed to go on with my work but I had lost confidence, backbone. I had gone soft. And then there were the recurring dreams. I asked Alma, "Do you think I was in any way to blame for what happened to Mrs. Wilde?"

She shocked me when she said, "Yes."

I sat upright in bed. "Yes? You think so?"

"No, *you* think so. You are so much a doctor of the mind, what of yours?"

"I have no control over nightmares. They come when they come."

"It is simply your conscience. Of course you ought to have taken her to Paris."

"But I couldn't cure the man! She would only have ended up more miserable."

She pulled the covers up about herself. It was a damp November, and even in my good solid room the London cold had seeped in. "Let me tell you something about yourself, Martin. I know your character so well. You are basically a kind man with a good heart. But like other men you are dogmatic, so certain that you know all the answers to what ails women."

"I dogmatic? *I?*"

"You know that she had the right to see her husband."

"Then what stopped her from seeing him? She could have seen him in Dieppe; she could have seen him at Nervi. Or at any given moment to take the Paris train."

"She could not do it alone. It was the office of a friend who loved her. Martin, let me give you a little lesson in theater. We each of us act according to our talent. Off the stage as well as on. She could accommodate his idiosyncrasies; he could not accommodate hers. In the end she felt that, with your help, she might try again, for both their sakes."

"It was too great a risk for a woman so ill."

"Was it? The truth, dear Martin, is in the body. I learned that from you. Look at yourself. Wretched, your health is suffering, and she cannot rest until you make it up to her."

"Don't tell me that you believe in vengeful spirits."

"No, but you do."

I turned away, but my mind would not turn away. She kissed and stroked my back and curled her warm body close to me. "And make it up to him."

"And how exactly, since you've become a doctor of the mind."

"Do what she wants you to do. Go to Paris. See if she was right. Could you have cured him? And if so, do what you can for him. If not, what would you have to lose, except your bad dreams."

"I'm considering the idea of emigrating to the States. Setting up a practice in New York and leave all of this behind me."

"You will not, not before you give her what she asks. Is it so much? Was she wrong about him, as you believe? Or was she right in which case you may have to bend that stiff back of yours and beg forgiveness. One or the other. Or else your ghosts will come across the ocean with you."

She was right of course. And yet I found reasons to delay. Legal matters with my father's estate, arrangements with a New York hospital where I might work until either I found a practice to take over or set up one of my own. And of course a competent doctor to take over my London practice.

It was a cold November of the new century when the last of the impediments were resolved. It was with actual dread that I sent a note to Ross, I confessed that I had been remiss in this matter of Wilde, and did he feel it inappropriately late for a visit to Paris? Was he certain Wilde would welcome speaking of his wife when so much time had passed.

"Fortuitous," he answered. "I heard from him this morning. He's ill, he can't pay the landlord, not even cigarette money for three days. He begged me to come over, but I'm needed, I have to settle my mother in Mentone, and one can never be entirely sure of Oscar's emergencies. If you could go as my emissary, I would be terribly obliged."

"You will arrange it, then."

"Actually I intended to carry a suit over to him, his clothes are becoming shabby and I've had one of his old ones let out for him. Let that be the excuse, then. And if you want to please him, bring him a bottle of Chateau Olivier and treat him to a good dinner. If he is as ill as he claims, I will go directly. Let me leave you my cable address."

"And except for you, he is totally alone and destitute."

Ross hesitated before he answered. "Yes and then, no. Friends drop in to see him whenever they are in Paris. He's had a terrible time with Harris, however. They had made some business arrangement, some piece of work Oscar had never finished, Oscar offered to sell him the plot and scenario, and then it seems that someone else has a claim on it. He fights over money. Begs money. He's possessed with the loss of it. Dear God, who can blame him. Go and see what he's up to."

And so, early November, harsh winter in all ways, I set out on my final voyage across the channel. The pitching waves, the cry of the gulls, passengers seasick over the side were metaphor for my state of mind.

We docked in a pouring rain. I was cold to the bone by the time I reached the train, and then a wet carriage ride through the Paris streets, everything tightly closed against the downpour, faint lights through clouded windows, steam from chimneys, wind whipping at the horse's mane and whistling against the side of the carriage.

And thus I arrived at last at the Hotel D'Alsace to meet Wilde face to face. Or heart to heart. God knew what I felt, or what I meant, or what was going on behind my eyes in the "unconscious," a concept with which I was fast losing sympathy. I just wanted it finished and to start a new life in a new country, an energetic new world where no one gave a damn about Oscar Wilde.

20

CHAPTER

*He had cleaned the knife many times, til there was
no stain left upon it. It was bright, and glistened. As
it had killed the painter, so would it kill the
painter's work. It would kill the past, and when that
was dead he would be free ... he would be at peace.*

Oscar Wilde, *The Picture of Dorian Gray*

Clutching my packages close to shield them from the rain, greatcoat flapping in the gusty wind, I found myself before a quite respectable hotel, certainly no hovel. I entered, wind at my back. Pages of the register on the counter caught the gust. I had to lean on the door to shut it. But I could not shut out my apprehension of this visit. I presented my card to the landlord and asked that it be sent up to M. Sebastian Melmouth.

Ah, was I the *docteur* from the Embassy? M. Wilde had been lying alone in bed all morning waiting for me. Very wicked to leave a man so *malade*. Now the wife came rushing out, drying her hands on her apron. The man was too ill to be left alone; she could not be expected to rush up there at every moment. Is this how the British treated their subjects? Madame Landlord preceded me up the stairs, scolding me all the way, led me to a door, knocked, opened it herself and let me in. I heard her mutter *"Honte,"* as she left, which, if I remembered my French, was *shame.*

The sitting room was empty. "Mr. Wilde?" These were evidently furnished rooms, but the apartment was spacious, the table covered with books and manuscripts, some of them still bound up, a handsome vase of flowers but the petals beginning to droop; they must have been there for some days. I saw a handsome silver flask, a set of small silver bottles of exquisite design; on the wall fine sketches. Begging money from friends and buying hot-house flowers? I set down my parcels, took off my coat and shook the rain out of it. Again I called, "Mr. Wilde?"

From the other room, his voice. "In here."

As I entered the bedroom the stench of infection assaulted me. They had implied downstairs that he was ill, but I was not prepared for what I saw.

Wilde lay on a disordered bed, florid face, belly distended under the stale sheet, the hands that lay on the sheet swollen, like hands of patients in the late stages of heart disease. He had become what they caricatured: the overlarge features, the St. Bernard eyes sloped down at the corners, the full mouth, but lips dry and cracked from fever. His ear was covered by a stale bandage with a yellowish discharge seeping through and staining the pillow. He looked the color of putty. Stupidly I said, "Mr. Wilde? I am Martin Frame, a friend of Robbie Ross. I have come to bring your suit."

"My suit?" A bark of a laugh which resolved into a rheumy cough. "When I am ready for the zinc bed?"

Zinc bed alluded to the morgue. In dismay I blurted out, "What on earth has happened here?"

He tried to shift his weight. His hand went to his ear. He gasped in pain. "They operated yesterday. I have finished the medicine he gave me and they were to be back this morning with the *panseur* to change the dressing. No one has come. I cannot get to the cable office to tell Robbie."

"He couldn't know you were so ill. I'll cable for you."

He nodded his thanks. But his face was a mask of tragedy, a man totally lost to circumstance. I had seen it before. Half the pain from the ravages of the infection, the rest in disgust at the nauseating smell, the fouled pillow and the rumpled sweated sheets. I took off my coat and rolled up my sleeves "Fortunately, I'm a doctor as well as a messenger. If you would permit me."

I touched his forehead. The man was burning with fever. I poured him a glass of water and steadied his hand so that he could drink it. He fell back helplessly against the pus-stained pillow. "Thank you," he said.

Where to wash? On a corner table stood a basin of water and a much-used towel. The water was cold, the soap had been left to dissolve in the bowl. Disgusting. Distastefully I washed my hands and dried them on my pocket handkerchief.

"Have you a housekeeper?"

"A Spanish Rosa who does the rooms."

I went out to the landing and called down the stairs. "Rosa! *S'il vous plait, de l'eau chaude!* What the blazes was French for soap. "Soap!" I called down, "towels and clean linen."

Carefully I took off the stale bandage which stuck with a yellow glue to his skin. The stench assailed me. In the ear was a wad of putrid cotton wool which held in the discharge. This I carefully extracted, and set the soiled dressings out of sight and smell. The Rosa I had called for, a big-boned country girl, walked in apprehensively, carrying a bowl of steaming water and a cloth, but refused to come close, as if the man in the bed were a leper. She quickly set down the bowl and fled. "Let me wash the ear and we'll let it drain a bit. It may relieve the pain."

I had seen Wilde many times before. At the theater, taking his curtain call, tall, elegant, smugly self-satisfied. On the street a few times, knowing that eyes were following him in admiration, or dismay; I supposed that he enjoyed that also. And the glimpse of him at the Cadogan. Now, to see him like this. To whatever place I may have, in anger, consigned him that day in Genoa, I knew he was almost there. This careless husband from whose ear dripped a yellow pus; I knew that the yellow ochre was like the bright fungus on a dead tree. The worst of it was inside, eating at him. If Alma Belmont had sent me to a confessional, in truth I had come not for a *mea culpa* but to vindicate myself. Now that I was here, seeing him so lost, if I had known nothing of his history, he might have stirred my compassion.

Carefully I washed the ear. The warm water must have been soothing.

A wan smile. Even that cost him some pain. "You are St. Martin come to help the poor and suffering."

"I? You have the wrong man. Saint, I am not." To which *she* heartily concurred with a wind tap to the window.

I found fresh bandages in a cabinet and dressed the ear, but lightly to avoid any pressure that might cause him pain. He put his hot hand on my hand. "I am most grateful." The voice from the ruined body was unexpectedly melodious.

It was the landlord's wife herself who brought the fresh linen. She was prepared to be annoyed at the inconvenience but when she saw him in that putrid bed, she was deeply affected. "Ah, *pauvre monsieur!*" and went screaming to the landing at the housemaid who had neglected, probably out of fear, to change the linen.

She inspected the logistics of her task. "A few moments in the chair, if *Monsieur* can manage?"

"That would be a relief," he said. "I am quite drowning in this bed."

She pulled back the covers. His nightshirt was damp and stained with drops of dried blood and yellow pus. I thought, the man wanted only color and light. Well, he had color, at least. Constance shrieked at me with the wind coming through some chink in a badly fixed window pane. In the clothes cupboard Madame Landlord found him a fresh nightshirt. She was no stranger to naked middle aged men. She helped him up. He stood unsteadily, a hand to my shoulder. Nothing delicate, she pulled off his stained garment and pulled on the clean nightshirt. Now I saw his eyes turn down, searching for something under the bed. She, pulling soiled sheets from the bed, nudged it out with her shoe. The chamber pot. She deftly spread the cleaned pressed sheets on the bed, changed the pillowcase, gathered the soiled linen in her arms, and begged forgiveness for the discomfort of the bed and promised to bring up some soup for *pauvre monsieur.*

The bath and "convenience" were probably down the hall, I couldn't walk him there, and his dead wife stood over my shoulder, accusing me. If others flagellated for their sins, my penance was to hold the pot while Wilde took a piss. "This gesture alone, dear boy, will assure you a seat in heaven." He nodded toward the cupboard. "My robe. Perhaps I will sit for a bit." A handsome robe but showing wear. He tied the belt with trembling fingers, ran a hand through his disordered hair with unexpected vanity, and with my help, lowered himself into the armchair beside the bed. A sigh of relief. "Now that you have saved my life, do not let her drown me in soup. There is half a bottle of good wine in my clothes cupboard. And glasses in the other room."

"I'm also a messenger from Bacchus. Allow me."

"The ear roars like a river," he called. "I thought I was being carried along into the River Styx. If you hadn't come, I would have put coins over my eyes and waited for the boatman."

The glasses were good crystal. For a man in penury, he managed to live well enough. I filled his glass with wine but mine with whiskey I had brought for myself. I needed something stronger to survive this interview. He took the wine with an unsteady hand. He brought it to his nose, a smile of recognition. "Ahhh..." and then another more heartfelt, "Ahhh! Robbie must have told you. How *enormously* kind of you." He sipped, savored it, but took it down at a swallow, the connoisseur yielding to the man in pain, more anesthetic than aesthetic. I filled the glass again.

"Has she sent you, then?"

"She?"

"Constance. Robbie wrote to me. Last night as I lay here alone and in pain, I thought I saw her watching me." A hand to his forehead unsteadily. "I think she would be very sad to see me like this." He held out the glass to be refilled. "And so she sent you as an angel of mercy."

No, mercy was not my strong point. I took my whiskey as he had taken his wine. Too much too fast. The heat of it went directly to my head.

"At the end she wished me dead, you know."

I pulled a chair beside his, refilled my glass "Why should you think that?"

"She must have told you. I had become a beggar. My allowance often came late. I was desperate and I suppose it annoyed her. I hadn't a shilling. I wrote to her asking for my few pounds. She answered me with a terrible letter, the first cruel word she had ever written. I had the letter with

me when Mellor invited me to Switzerland. Do you know
the man?

His hand trembled. I took the wine from him. "Would
you like to lie down now?"

He stopped me with a gesture. "I have been lying here
all night, having long conversations with the figures on the
wallpaper." A hand to his brow, which he let drop to his
lap. "We were speaking of ..."

"Someone named Mellor."

"Mellor. Robbie knows him. Silent, dull, cautious, and
economical. But I had no choice, you see. When invited, it
meant a bed, and Mellor set a good table. In the letter she
said nothing about her illness, although her friends had
told me." He passed a hand near his forehead and then let
it drop to his lap. "Switzerland was dreadful, I longed for
Italy where the sunset flushes like a rose, but I could not
escape. I had nothing to pay my fare back. I read and
reread her letter. 'I forbid you to come to me,' she said. 'I
forbid you to go to him in Italy. I forbid you to go back to
your filthy ways.' And Mellor refused me money, and so I
had to borrow it from one of his servants. When I returned
to Paris, I found a letter from her. She was going into
surgery the following morning. All anger had left her. Do
you think she knew she might not survive? It was a lovely
letter. I wept at receiving it." His eyes glazed with tears. "I
saw her grave last year. An extraordinary view from that verdant hillside. And the stone, a simple cross in good taste, a
fine leaf pattern in green. My name not on it, of course. My
name would never have got her into heaven."

"She thought you destitute and alone. So indeed you
still visit friends."

"What are left of them. Robbie and Frank and now Frank
has tried to cheat me. I still have many friends in Europe
but now that I cannot work ... odd ..." He asked for his
glass, I refilled it, he took a sip and set it on the side table.
"I used to rely on personality. It was a fiction. Position drew
them, and once that was gone, they disappeared, the most

of them. I only wanted a little place near Genoa. The chastity of Switzerland had quite got on my nerves. In Italy one can live well for a few shillings a day. Sunlight counts as half one's income. But she would not see me." He leaned toward me, winced at the pain in the ear, half-brought a hand up to it. "Dear boy, what was it you wished to say to me? Why have you come? My good fortune of course, but I am curious."

Excellent question. How did I begin to answer it.

"A wake, perhaps. You know that I was not invited to the funeral. I had to mourn her alone. Perhaps you have come to help me do that now."

The whiskey had given me Dutch courage. "Wilde, I was treating her in Genoa. Her back and her legs caused her great pain. Yet she spoke of nothing but you, and with great affection."

"And you found that difficult to believe? There was always a deep affection between us."

"In truth?"

A snort of a laugh. "I am standing at the brink, dear boy. Some poor angel stands behind me with my list of sins. He would tolerate nothing less than truth."

"Then in truth, I thought it a marriage of convenience since you had this ...this .."

"Dual nature? You were mistaken. She had violet eyes, thick coils of chestnut hair that made her head droop like a blossom." A hand to the ear; it must have pained him terribly. " I was rushing about the world giving my lectures, some of them successful, sometimes I would find myself speaking to seated bodies in the final stages of rigor mortis. I needed a home. And she was beautiful and bright. She knew French and Italian, she had the good taste to adore my poetry, and she had a small income, enough to permit me to begin writing in earnest."

"I should have called that marriage a convenience."

"Have you been speaking to Shaw? He never saw the beauty in Constance. Trust me, I was impossibly in love with her. Marriage was new to me then. I had known women, of course, but a first marriage is a thrill."

"First. But she never divorced you."

"My second marriage was all the more passionate." He gestured for his glass to be refilled. As I offered it to him, he put his hand on my arm, rested it there for a moment, and then an almost affection squeeze. I pulled my hand sharply away, sloshing the wine.

"Ah, then that answers my question."

"What question."

"You are a friend of Robbie's. And those eyes of yours and the soft beard, and the air of youthful tragedy."

"*I* have an air of tragedy? What nonsense."

"Trust me that it is true. And so I wondered whether you were Uranian. Just between us," he lowered his voice. "I will take your secret to the grave, which may be sooner than one would wish."

"I assure you that I am not." I hadn't meant the protest to sound so fierce.

Those sloping brows raised. I may have blushed. I felt hot under the collar.

"You know that I was never a sodomite, if that is what disturbs you. And under the circumstances you are safe with me. In any case, half of what they accused me of was untrue."

I would have blurted out, *and the other half was?* Alma Belmont was in my ear, scolding me. I carefully rephrased my tone. "And the other half... was it?"

"Are you asking to hear intimate details of the other half?"

I flushed hot. "Not at all; that wasn't what I meant."

For a man who had lived what sort of life in the last few years I could scarcely imagine, he had an inordinately gentle smile. "My young friend, trust me. Your interest may be more than simple curiosity. If it stimulates you to speak about it, you will go back to your rooms tonight and be very nervous about your own sexuality. And a little adventurous. If so, remember you have friends in Paris."

I had no words to answer him.

"Martin, may I call you Martin?" I nodded yes, and took down a gulp of whiskey to cover my discomfort. "Martin, when one needs to be loved, simply being held and kissed is passionate enough. I adored Constance, if that was your question. I loved being held and kissed by her. She was heaven itself. Her voice was soft as an Italian night. You may not know it to see her, but she was in her way a seductive woman. I thought that she and I would make the perfect modern couple. I misjudged her."

"How so?"

"She had a little French, a little Italian, she was well-read but she lacked stage presence."

"Meaning what exactly?"

He shifted a little in his chair, a hand toward his ear, wincing in pain. "When an actor walks out onto a stage, the audience wants nothing so much as to like him. If he makes a mistake, he has only to keep his head, make some joking excuse and move on. But if he allows himself to be embarrassed, if he flounders, if he discomforts his audience, he is lost. They will reject him. She should have stood next to me, equal to me. She could not."

I wanted to say, how bloody egoistic. But it was probably true.

"I was the Lord of Language. I had a position and a reputation. She was a generous hostess, but when it came to conversation, she was lost. Yet when we were alone, I loved making love to her. She was quite wonderful."

"And she gave you beautiful children."

The tragic mask, softened by wine and conversation, reformed itself. "You have come to speak of my wife. I would rather not speak of the children."

No, I would suppose not.

He signaled for the glass to be refilled. "Martin, why have you come?"

Fair question. "I came simply to tell you that, at the end, she spoke of the happy early years of your marriage, the home she adored and her happiness in it."

"That was truth itself. We were both deliriously happy. And desperately in love. We found a wonderful house. No, it was more than a house. It was a home such as no one had seen before. Beauty around each corner; each little alcove a surprise for the eye." His hand fluttered toward his brow. "She had such a sense of design with her clothes, I surely thought ideas would spring from her lovely brow. But she had not the magical touch of the creative. I made that house my canvas. The yellows and blues, a touch here, a marvelous Italian tile there. To her mind no great shapes or colors came. I asked her, Dearest, what shall you have of your own? And she said, Find me an aesthetic bath." At this his mind seemed to drift. His soft eyes turned toward me, as if to beg understanding. "She must have been terribly hurt when she lost the house. I could not have imagined the depth of Queensbury's hatred of me. He struck at me and wounded her."

"I would guess she was more devastated by the loss of her husband, and that happened long before the house went to the creditors."

"It was my work, you see. I was away a great deal. She resented me for it."

"On the contrary, she seemed to understand."

"She did not understand. She was terribly hurt. I used the excuse of her pregnancy, but actually I wanted to enjoy my friends and she dulled the conversation. I could not be myself with her. And that was the truth of it. She became what she most abhorred, a domestic woman."

"She was married. She was a domestic woman."

"She made a career of it. The budget. The price of boots. Bargaining. I detest bargaining. When we were first engaged, I was interviewed by that horror of an aunt. She said to me, 'I hope, Mr. Wilde, that you have sufficient income to support my niece. She is not terribly thrifty.' I thought, how excellently she and I will get along: careless, thriftless and in love. But the moment we married, she became the spirit of domestic economy. I spent money as I spent money. I am what I am. She ought to have realized it and accepted it."

"And so you left her alone a great deal. And yet she excused you. Why, if you don't mind speaking of it."

"Why should she not? She was a virgin when I married her. She had lovemaking which would never have been equaled by men of her set. She had her home and her children, and I had the demands of my own work."

"... and she did not understand your work."

"She understood nothing. But she was a good woman, always loving, always kind, wonderful to the children. I do not excuse myself. I am just stating the fact."

"So you went about your life and she stayed at home."

"My life was so rich and varied. I had my friends, my work, my little pleasures."

"You mean your vices?"

Those bleared eyes, the furrowed brow. He was searching out my meaning. "I was a poet. My life was rich in sensation."

"And one's obligations to one's wife?"

"I respected her. I attended her parties. I went shopping with her on the boulevard. She could have made a varied life of her own, but she was so terribly attached."

"... attached ..."

"... like a sea anemone. If only she could have come to me and said, I understand your need for adventure and experience; well I am the same. What would you say if I took a lover? I would have been overjoyed. Life was there for the taking, and in the end she chose to become what she had run from."

His glass was empty. I filled it again. "May I ask an utterly personal question?"

"How more personal can you get than the piss-pot, dear boy. And conversation is all that keeps me from despair. You want after all to hear about my sexual adventures?"

"She said that you left her bed because an infection recurred."

"That was true. But it was also a good excuse. I could no longer make love with her."

"You'd discovered the pleasures of homosexual life."

"I had discovered those pleasures long before then."

"Then why didn't you simply admit it to her and divorce her? Free her before the trial and all that public circus?"

"Ah, that." He turned his head. His eyes fluttered, a hand went to his lips. "I fell in love," he said, "if you in your conventional view of the world can understand what it means to fall totally and absolutely and deliciously in love."

"But you must have known he was a disaster in your life."

"Of course I saw it. I tried more than once to separate from him. I knew that if my passion went deeper, I would be drowned in it. He was selfish, petulant, careless with gifts, leaving my letters about. Poor careless Bosie."

"Good God, man, what prevented you from letting go of him."

"I cannot say." A glaze of tears. "Is she really gone? I can almost sense her watching me. She could never leave me this way. She might even ask them to admit me to her heaven." He looked to the wine bottle which was almost empty and held out his glass again. "Alas, my book of life has been sent for advance notices to the other place. Shall I go to heaven or to hell. What do you think?"

"I'm a scientist. I leave heaven and hell to the poets."

"If they read my poetry," he said, "then they will surely send me to heaven. But she will be there in silken wings, watching me with those proscriptive eyes ...and if I go to hell, there will be beautiful boys but it will be hotter than Algiers. Bosie and I were there, and so I know what hell is. Did Robbie tell you that Bosie has been resurrected? He is thinking of going back to London. I told him that it was too soon. He ought to wait until he is sixty. But you know his mother."

"Was the marriage over, then, once you had met Douglas?"

"I lived with my wife, shall I say on and off, until the end. Did Robbie tell you that I had spent Christmas with the family just before the trial? He was there."

"What I don't understand ..." He asked for more wine, the bottle was empty, I went for his bottle in the clothes cupboard. "What I cannot understand is how a man as honest as you seem to be could have been so duplicitous with her."

"In what way, duplicitous?"

I filled my glass with whiskey. "To have pretended to keep the marriage alive, and to be passionately in love with another man."

"One thing had nothing to do with the other. But I was indeed a passionate man and I needed love of another sort. You surely can understand that."

"I understand duty and honor."

"I understand beauty and the freedom to explore the deepest part of the human soul."

"We're not animals to go rutting with every burst of passion."

"How could you know, dear boy, since you have never tasted any of it."

My manhood bristled. "I assure you that I've had my share of sexual pleasure."

"Not even scratched the surface. Like an Englishman who eats his beef and sprouts and has never tasted truffles and a delicate flan."

"Oh, I think that if you would ask a certain actress back in London, you might think differently."

"I would guess that if you asked her, she would say that you were sexual as a stud horse is sexual, but that you knew nothing of true lovemaking. Do you mind my saying it? I am a good judge of men on that subject."

I did mind. I resented it. I took a swallow of whiskey and my woozy mind went back to my Miss Belmont. She did not support me. *You were dogmatic even in your lovemaking.*

"... then after the first years she was simply a convenience."

"To have a house was convenient. A wife was convenient. I was ill, she was there. I needed my mail to be sent to a hotel, she was there. And she showed no inclination to divorce me."

"She needed grounds for divorce. Did she ever suspect that she had grounds?"

"I cannot honestly say what my wife suspected."

"You could have made the noble gesture, given her grounds and her freedom."

"She did not ask for her freedom."

"Then knowing that she was still your wife and that you had two sons who needed unsullied names, why in God's earth did you start that impossible libel suit?"

"I did not think it impossible. It was to save my family name that I began it."

"How did you expect to win the suit when you were guilty?"

"Guilty of what? They accused me of corrupting boys. I corrupted no one. Those boys were renters."

"Very thin line between temptation and corruption. You gave gold cigarette cases to boys of a lower class. How could they resist?" I finished my glass and refilled it. I I was feeling the heat of the whiskey. I loosened my collar, stretched out my legs. "I wish I could understand what pleasure a man like yourself, forgive me, a corpulent man of your age ..."

"Forty six is no great age."

"Forty six, a body in wretched condition, and a young boy barely out of puberty. What was the point of it?"

"If you have never felt it, I could never explain it to you."

"Why not? Aren't you the Lord of Language?"

He laughed, with his whole body in spite of the pain it must have caused him. "How glad I am you came. There must be a God after all. I could not bear to lie here alone and in pain. I am certain now that she sent you to me."

I was damned drunk and at that moment I suspected that it might very well have been true.

"How," he began, "can I describe lying beside a young god just born from the eye of Venus, unsullied, every line of him exquisite poetry. And the warm sexuality and the excitement of the first touch of his fingers ... shall I go on?"

"No."

"I thought not. You would drown in it."

"And you never saw the wrong in it?"

"Bankers and lawyers are out in broad daylight cheating and plundering widows and orphans. Society says nothing. But to find that I frequented these houses of innocent pleasure, that infuriated them. And there I was on the stand, accused."

"And you went back to your wife for help."

"What would you have done? Martin, she could have divorced me ten times over. She did not."

"She loved you."

To that no reply.

"That night when you asked her out to the theater together with your lover..."

"Pure exploitation. She ought not to have done it." He reached into a bedside drawer for a packet of cigarettes, small aromatic cigarettes of an expensive brand. And he had no money for food? He tried to find matches but had no energy. I found some on the bedside table, lit one for him. He drew in smoke, wincing at the pain to his ear. He offered me one. I took it. And we smoked and drank, two men at a private club. And one of us was sick with guilt and the other was, very possibly, dying.

"So you had a deep and passionate love for this rotter Douglas and yet in prison you begged her forgiveness."

"I was on the rack. What else could I have done? And I was genuinely contrite."

"Contrite in that you regretted your homosexuality?"

"Contrite that in pursuing my own pleasures, I had inadvertently hurt her. And hurt myself in that I had compromised my art. My art was my life. It was my art Bosie took from me with his enormous hate of his father. I was guilty of being guileless in the face of that venomous anger. If you cannot understand the richness and depth of sexual pleasure, I was altogether unable to comprehend the power of his hatred for his father. I was in prison, wounded in spirit almost to the death. Eating filth that gave me dysentery. Defecating in a pail that stood in my cell until morning. Walking the silent yard, forbidden to speak with other prisoners. Bosie had done this to me with his selfishness and his tantrums. I blamed him and I knew that only she could help me get out of it."

"So you used her."

"No more than she used me."

"How on earth did she use you?"

"The moment they had me, she had control of me."

"In what way?"

"As she wanted me. Passive, agreeable, submissive, contrite. And in that hell of a prison, all I could think of was coming home, being sheltered. What would you have said?"

"And yet you argued in prison, over money I think it was."

"Did she tell you that?" He started in alarm. "Did she believe them?" The ear must have been throbbing. He let out an involuntary moan, took the cigarette between his fingers, began to put it out, thought better of it, licked at his dry lips and drew in smoke again. He held out his hands to me. "Look at my hands. I wrote a wonderful hand. Now they tremble; you can scarcely read my writing. I cannot think clearly. Ideas do not come as they did. Even in prison, at the worst of it, images still came into my head. And my fingers itched to write them. I had no more than to sit down with the pen and words flowed. But now, I go to dinner with a friend and there, at the next table, is a woman who, before the trial, fought for my invitation. She sits there with her son who has just finished his school term and is being taken on the grand tour. She sees me. I only nod my head and smile and she snatches the boy away as if I am a vampire. I sit down to write, there is nothing in my head. I must be loved, you see. Now I am a leper. "

"... we were speaking of the prison argument ..."

"My friends knew that I would have nothing to live on. And my sons would always be taken care of. Had they inherited the money, I, their father, a pauper, would have had to come begging from his own children. I could not bear the thought of it."

"Then you knew and did not protest."

He turned his head to the side, touching the bad ear as one keeps putting a tongue on a sore tooth. "I knew and protested but they went ahead with it, and it was the ruin of my friendship with my wife. Until then she wrote often. Then the letters stopped, and it took a long while before the anger left her. If indeed it ever did." He held out the cigarette and watched the smoke curl upward. "Martin, do you understand what it means to love beauty and to have known ugliness?"

"Ugliness? I would have thought that until the trial you lived a charmed life."

"My father was a surgeon. He was a grand story teller and a wonderful fisherman. But do you know what I remember of him? He was unclean, his nails, sometimes his clothes. It disgusted me. I had a sister I adored and she died as a child. The pain of that loss still stabs at me. From my father's other, shall I call it ... relationship, I had two stepsisters, quite lovely girls. They went to a dance, stood too close to the fire, the hem of the dress of one of them caught fire, the other tried to put it out and they were horribly burned to death. Their brother was my father's true son. He inherited from my father. My own brother was a drunkard. I had nothing of love from him. When I needed to come home during the trial, he refused me. My dear mother whom I loved immoderately, did you see her before her death? Hiding from the world in those ridiculous veils. That was my life, Martin. And I swore, I promised myself early on, that I would never know pain or sorrow or ugliness. That I would surround myself with beauty. Can you understand that?"

"Frankly? Not at all. I believe in responsibility."

"... and in God's commandments. Would it surprise you to know that when I left prison I asked to be accepted into a monastery? I was ready to exchange my prison cell for a monk's cell. But they asked me if I accepted unconditionally the infallibility of God. I had to be honest. No, I said, if it means that man was created in God's image. I was, of course, thinking of lawyers. My wife, however, was devout."

"So she said."

"And you. Are you a believer if not in beauty then in some passionate thing?"

"I believe in standing by one's choices. We make them and live by them. If a man takes a wife, he takes care of that wife. And he guards his children from harm. If he doesn't, well, he bears the burden of guilt."

"My dear Martin, what burden of guilt brings you here to me?"

I had forgotten that I was speaking with a writer, a man who had plumbed the passions of the human soul, understanding all but his own. He caught me unprepared to lie. I blurted out, "I was treating your wife for an ailment I supposed to be partly in her mind. She seemed to improve and she asked me to bring her to you. I judged it to be the wrong decision. I refused her."

He fell back deeply into his chair. "Ahhhh ..."

My drunken tongue was loosed. "We live by our decisions, Wilde. You decided to make a stupid lawsuit when you must have known your children would suffer. She decided to send the children back to school, and she may have ruined your chances of reconciliation. How could you have reconciled when you didn't understand responsibility? There is sex and there is love and there is the moral question of protecting one's children. I saw all that, and I made a decision." I turned away. "And like you, I must stand by it." I felt hot tears spring to my eyes. Drunken tears. I covered my eyes with my hands.

I felt his touch to my knee. "Dear boy," he said. "Of what use is regret. Life is what it is."

"All I saw was that you'd left her in pain. You had run off with this rotter and for some ... some specter of momentary pleasure, you abandoned your wife and children. That I found inexcusable."

"And do you excuse a physician who has sworn to do no harm, when he refuses to bring a patient to Paris to see her desperate husband, and now comes with gifts of wine, begging for absolution?" I started to rise in protest. He waved me to be seated. "Which, dear boy, I give most absolutely. We are what we are, Martin. As God designed us. I do believe in God, you see."

"But not His commandments."

"As to that, in philosophy I am antinomian."

My head buzzed with the whiskey. "Meaning what? I'm not literary."

"I trust my own mind to tell me what is right or wrong."

"Does that make you your own God?"

"Or my own devil. My wife and I believed in the stars. We had our hands read. She had great faith in a certain Mrs. Robinson. But had the woman ever truly seen the lines of my hand, she would have wept for me."

He coughed and the cough persisted and hurt his ear as it shook him. I poured him a glass of water. He burned with fever. I brought a cold cloth and placed it on his forehead. With his hot fat hand, he grasped mine. Intimate. Begging respite from despair. Someone to be with him there on the brink. There was no guile in it.

Madame Landlord knocked and brought in a tureen of soup and some bread. And a note from a Dr. Tucker, expressing his regret for not coming sooner. An emergency at the hospital. He would stop by shortly. I knew that the doctor would undoubtedly give him an opiate. But I still had questions unanswered. These were final moments, I knew it was cruel of me to take this desperate advantage. But I asked, "Wilde, you chose the libel suit above your concern for your children. You must know that. Have you tried to see them since she died, to explain and beg their forgiveness?"

Now, the room felt too warm, and his presence too intense. I wanted to get out of there into the cold November air. And he knew it. And he also knew that if I left, he would be alone. So my question was pure blackmail.

"I have asked to see my children. I have written to them, but did not know where to send the letters."

"I find that hard to believe. You had the courage to break the laws of your country, to follow your own passion when it meant certain disgrace, and yet you couldn't play the detective and root out the whereabouts of your sons?"

"I hadn't the money to buy a decent dinner; how on earth could I go searching for my children. And tell me, if I had found them, what could I have said? And if I could have explained, what if they detested me. It was she who should have explained it to them. And she did not."

"She expected to see you at Nervi."

"I expected to see her at Dieppe. But she was ill. I was asked to wait. And I waited and waited. I expected to see her at Nervi, but still she asked me to wait."

"You didn't believe that she was genuinely ill."

"On the contrary. I had no doubt that she was ill. And so I waited. I longed to see the children. " He turned his face away. "I used to walk the prison yard trying to picture my sons. I realized then that one hair of my sweet Cyril's head was worth all of Bosie who understood love not at all. I only survived thinking of the moment I would see my sons again. How I would be standing at the prison gate, and Vyvyan holding Constance by the hand and Cyril standing shyly behind her skirts, and Vyvyan would come running to me, and Cyril afraid to leave his mother's side, and I holding my arms open to him and at last, unable to restrain the great love he had for me, he would come running toward me. And how I would try to explain. And then she sent me pictures of the boys, two sweet angels in little Eton jackets. I thought, it will be now; this is my true release from that hell of a prison. Martin, I waited and I waited. I waited two months, three. Can you understand the terrible desperation of a man like myself who had been scorned, despised. I needed to be held and to be loved.

And finally the letter came. Yes, she would see me. But she had decided to send the children back to school. She was sending away my children! If the gods had punished me before, now they sent the final bolt of lightning. I was bereft. I felt I would never see them again. I gave such a cry that I had never done in prison, never in the most painful hour. To have lost my children was to have lost paradise." He pushed himself out of the chair. Before I could catch him, his knees buckled and he sank to the floor." I fell to my knees, I raised my hands to the heavens, and I begged God to take the memory of my sons away from me. Knowing that I would never see them again was more than I could bear."

With great effort, I lifted him. He was a heavy man. Clumsily, I got him onto the bed, out of his robe, lifted his legs, drew the covers over them, and settled him on the clean pillow.

He turned to me, held onto me with a beggar's hand to my arm. "And I went back to Douglas. Where else had I to go? He was the only one who wanted me. But she would not have it. She stopped my allowance."

"Good lord, man, can you blame her?"

"Yes, I blamed her. She drove me back to him. She wrote me dreadful letters. If I went back to that beast, she would see to it that I never had a shilling from her again. Violent letters such as I had never had from her. And what did Bosie give me but love and affection. And had she not given me that allowance freely? What right had she to tell me how to spend it? If I had chosen to buy tobacco instead of bread, she would have said nothing. But as it was, I used it to take him to dinner."

"And you find that honorable?"

"What has honor to do with love? A man can live without honor; without love he is dead. Some time ago, I was in desperate straits and Robbie sent me a few pounds. I met a poor boy who desperately wanted a bicycle. I bought it for him. Can you understand that?"

"Absolutely not. Why couldn't he work and buy himself a bicycle? And the money was given to you for a specific reason."

"Try ... *try* to understand me. See a field of marguerites. Is there rule and design to explain their beauty?"

"Since you wanted fields of marguerites and that ass Douglas, why expect her to do anything for you?"

"Because I needed her." He put his palms to his eyes.

"So Douglas doesn't love you now."

"... tolerates me. We still have a good conversation now and then."

When he took his hands from his eyes, I saw what desperation was. I saw the abysmal bottom of despair, but I had to have an answer to my terrible question. Or else I would be haunted by her forever. "Wilde..."

He held up his swollen hand; he touched his brow. "I cannot think any more. Nothing seems to come. I was so wild with ideas. I was a rushing river. Now I am dry. It seems inconceivable."

"... Wilde, if she could have come to you in Paris then .."

"My friends come to Paris from time to time. We have a good dinner and a talk. Esterhazy was here a few days ago. Robbie comes. Harris used to come, but he is angry with me. I forget why." His eyes drifted, inward, away from the pain and the fever and the hopelessness. "Once, it was the last time I had dinner at home, it was Christmas, I think. Robbie was there. Did I speak of it earlier? The boys were playing in my smoking room. They adored the empty cigarette boxes I left in the waste paper baskets and they hunted for those like treasures, and the wallpaper, and I had exquisite paper with little raised bubbles in the pattern and when I was not watching, they loved to poke fingers in the bubbles and pop them; and then Vyvyan saw my walking stick and asked, could he have it, and I told him when he was tall enough to use it, he might have the thing. I returned to my reading and I heard laughter and the two scamps, they came back into the room, Vyvyan, with books tied under his feet so that he was taller and could manage the stick. And once, once when they were very young and Constance and I were giving a dress ball and we had marvelous costumes made for them. They were to appear as two little lords Fauntleroy, which they detested. Cyril wanted a navy suit of real navy cloth; we insisted on the costumes and they ran out and the two of them took off all their clothes and came running in stark naked. Constance was scandalized but I thought it exquisitely charming. They got their navy suits. Now, I cannot write to them; they have no mother to hold them and kiss them. What will become of them? If I think of it, I will go mad."

He closed his eyes and seemed to fall asleep.

I heard the tapping at the door, and the footsteps enter. The doctor. I went out to meet him, introduced myself as a friend from London, also a physician. He was an affable sort, a Doctor Tucker. We exchanged London medical gossip. And then without consulting me, this was, of course, his patient, he opened his bag, took out his needle, filled it. "He is in great pain. He no longer responds to morphia so I have been giving him some opium and chloral. I hated to give him an injection while the infection is still draining."

"How bad is the infection?"

He held up a hand, walked into Wilde's room, came out directly with the needle empty. "Your friend has taken a turn for the worse. I warned him months ago that he must stop drinking. He refuses to hear it. Some days ago he went out in bad weather and drank himself sick with absinthe. After the surgery last night, he began to ramble. He wants his friends to find him a small chalet, in the cup of the hills, he says, where he can work in peace. I don't think he has worked for quite a long while, poor man. And then he sings. Sad, that brilliant mind is most certainly going."

"He seemed clearheaded, at least part of the time."

"He wanders in and out of it. Sometimes lucid, sometimes lost in memory."

"So the infection is that far gone? Is it meningitis?"

"... what?"

"Meningitis, then?"

"Oh yes," he said thoughtfully, "we will certainly put meningitis on the death certificate when the time comes. You can tell his family. Rest assured." He leaned closer. "But my friend, between us ..."

The tone of the voice, the nod of the head, the implication of "wandering mind" could only mean tertiary syphilis.

"Haven't you seen the rash on his palms? Around the nose? It is all over his back. What a pity for a man of his talents to suffer like this. You might mention to the family that the *panseur* should be paid, and the anesthetist for the surgery on the ear. The landlady showed me a bill for fifteen pounds. I was tempted to pay for it myself. It is a privilege to tend the man. I am fond of the theater. I have spent happy hours laughing at his clever lines. He is terribly funny. But I suppose that is at an end."

I cannot describe my state of mind as I reentered the room. His eyes were open now, more peaceful, the opiate beginning its work. He beckoned me to come and sit with him. "I forbid you to go to Naples, she said. I forbid you to come to me in Genoa. I forbid you to go back to your filthy habits." He looked fearfully about the room as if she were there. "Christ would never have tolerated Bosie. I was the only one who could handle him when he got into his fearful temper." He reached out to me, like a man drowning. "I married three times, you know. Once to a woman ..."

I took his hand and held onto it tightly, keeping him for a few moments more in this world. And what he did was to reach over with his other hand and lay it on my hand, in gesture of affection, or desperation.

And joined to him in this intimate way, I asked him my own desperate question. "Just tell me this ..."

He moved his head from side to side, as if to escape something.

"Had I brought her to Paris two years ago, could you have made a life with her? Would you have been able to give up the pretty boys and settle down to a domestic life?"

Had he heard me? He released me, lay back, smiling as if in another dimension of time. "Beauty is my vice, you see. Is Maurice coming to me? I only want the touch of his hand to calm me, but he has gone somewhere." He looked suddenly about the room, searching. "I miss my dear Neopolitans. I miss the brown faun with his woodland eyes and his sensuous limbs." I prayed that her spirit was in the room to hear this confession and to understand that I had been right. A leopard did not change his spots.

She answered me in the wind that screeched against the windows. The heavens opened, a downpour of rain descended and darkened the room. I lit the lamp. Its glow did not penetrate the mortal gloom. My heart was a rock. What was left of my theory of the "unconscious" sat sourly in my breast.

You see, how could I be sure of what he had said, or what I *assumed* he had said. The man had a way with words. He used them beyond their intrinsic meaning; to create an effect. That was his way of dealing with a difficult world. But what lay behind the words? What if I had peeled him away as I had peeled her, layer by layer? Ross had said it: Wilde was a gentle man, blaming only himself. But somewhere there had to be anger, bitterness, fury at the fates which had destroyed him. Where was the bile of regret inside the fragile heart? The body was disintegrating. Who would ever know the truth now? The matter went beyond homosexualism. He had fallen in love, God help him, with a rotter. He had given up the wife who had made a solid home for him and lost his beloved children. And when he realized his error, it was too late. He had nothing. He had lost his audience, his work, his prestige. What had he left to live for? Momentary sensation. A moment of drugged happiness with his brown faun with the woodland eyes and sensuous limbs. The terrible question was: Could anyone, even having solved the puzzle of this troubled heart whose legacy was to love "above the commonplace," could anyone have changed one critical decision? Where was logic in

these dark romances? Was logic simply banished along with
the solid mahogany and the dark velvet drapes? Or was the
ending to this romance fixed from the first moment the
eyes of a hurt girl, hungry for love, met the eyes of a brilliant poet whose need for public acclaim and hunger for
sensation overwhelmed him.

Wilde stirred, roused himself with effort, his eyelids
heavy with the drug, and began a conversation as if we had
never left it. "... and so you see, ill as I am, I cannot be
alone. Robbie has asked me to marry again, this time to a
nice middle-aged boy who can take care of me; but alas, I
am in love, with a beautiful fisherman. He is only eighteen."
He lay breathing heavily, eyes fluttering, the swollen hand
on the bedcover moving slightly as if the words that used to
come through those fingers were trying to resurrect.

I emptied my billfold and laid what money I had on his
bedside table.

As I left the room, I heard him singing, an opium dream,
some nonsensical drunken drug-dream gibberish. I was half
way down the stairs when, in my whiskey-soaked brain, I
heard her accusing voice: *You never listened! I talked my
heart out and you did not hear me!*

No, I hadn't listened. And standing there, listening now,
I realized that the tune he hummed was more than gibberish. With dread I climbed the stairs again. I opened his door
and leaned against it. The song ... it was the song he had
sung to his children, the one she had sung to me. From
those old days when he romped with his sons in the nursery. When he read them his stories. A song he had heard
from his own father. The song about the carp at the bottom
of the lake.

Athá mé in mu codladh, agus ná dúishe mé. I am
asleep, do not wake me.

And so I returned to my father's house in South
Kensington. And now I am packed for my emigration to
another country. I will finish this narrative and I will close

this notebook and seal it. It was my first and last case in the practice of the 'talking cure.' Leave it to the Austrian. Perhaps he will understand women better than I. And had I actually cured her? How can I know. When the heart fixes itself to one purpose, to an impossible dream, where is the cure? Could I have cured Wilde? From what? What was he searching for in those pretty boys? Some shadow of his own lost youth? If he had, as Ross suggested, made a life with a middle-aged "boy" who could have looked after him, if that was his sexual pattern, I might have understood him. But why the constant need for youth and beauty?

If one could change history. If Wilde had found the courage to meet her at Nervi. If they could have spoken together. If she could have been assured of his, if not physical love, then his devotion. If she could have made him a home in that little cup of the hills in Switzerland. If his children could once more have sat at their father's knee and been consoled.

And if I had been brilliant enough to understand the mysteries of the human heart.

I am, after all, only a doctor. I am not God.

As to Wilde, give the devil his due. He was a genius. I end this case history with one of his epigrams, from a collection I borrowed from Robbie Ross. Soap bubbles, these clever little lines. I choose the one that most aptly joins me with Wilde. He only wanted to be loved and he chose the only route that entirely circumvented it. I wanted to use my medical skill to save women and what I accomplished was, very possibly, to deprive English literature of what might have been his best work. As Wilde said:

There is no sin like stupidity.

As to Sherlock Holmes, he was only a fiction. Why didn't I know that?

Dr. Martin Frame. London, 1900

NOTE TO THE READER

From the time I read the *Letters of Oscar Wilde* many years ago, twelve hundred letters but only one written to his wife, my curiosity was piqued as to the true story of this marriage. And once I began my research at the Clark Library in Los Angeles, which has the largest Wilde collection, and read those of her letters still remaining (I suppose the family destroyed many, many were lost when the Tite Street house was pillaged, and some may still be in the hands of private collectors), I was convinced that the familiar story of Oscar Wilde's tragedy, especially concerning his wife's involvement after his release from prison, was incomplete.

In writing *The Case of the Pederast's Wife* I have used these letters, by her, to her, or by friends and family alluding to her, as signposts for the questions and answers, Martin functioning as my voice since those were the questions I would have wanted to put to her.

The story of her flight to Europe was described in the touching autobiography by Wilde's younger son, Vyvyan Holland, *The Son of Oscar Wilde*.

The scope of the novel did not permit me to touch on the third tragedy and probably the most poignant, the story of Wilde's older son, Cyril. In Mr. Holland's autobiography, he quotes a letter written by his older brother just before

Cyril went into battle in 1914. And with the kind permission of Merlin Holland, Oscar Wilde's grandson, I quote it here.

When I returned to England in 1898, I naturally realised our position more fully. Gradually I became obsessed with the idea that I must retrieve what had been lost. By 1900, it had become my settled object in life. All these years my great incentive has been to wipe that stain away; to retrieve, if it may be, by some action of mine, a name no longer honoured in the land. The more I thought of this, the more convinced I became that first and foremost, I must be a man. There was to be no cry of decadent artist, of effeminate aesthete, of weak-kneed degenerate.

To which his brother added:

My brother, pulling every string on which he could lay his hands, arranged for a transfer to a cavalry regiment in India which was going to France to fight ... he was killed on May 9, 1915, in what amounted to a duel with a German sniper.